The Tragic M

》》》》》》》》》》 《《《《《《《《《《

Lydia Zinovieva–Annibal

The Tragic Menagerie

TRANSLATED FROM THE RUSSIAN AND WITH

AN INTRODUCTION BY JANE COSTLOW

NORTHWESTERN UNIVERSITY PRESS
EVANSTON, ILLINOIS

》》》》》》》》》》 《《《《《《《《《《

Northwestern University Press

Evanston, Illinois 60208-4210

Originally published in Russian in 1907 under the title *Tragicheskii zverinets*.
English translation copyright © 1999 by Northwestern University Press.
All rights reserved.

Printed in the United States of America

ISBN 0-8101-1483-6

Library of Congress Cataloging-in-Publication Data

Zinovieva-Annibal, Lydia (Lidia Dmitrievna), 1866–1907.
   [Tragicheskii zverinets. English]
   The tragic menagerie / Lydia Zinovieva-Annibal ; translated
from the Russian by Jane Costlow.
      p.   cm. — (European classics)
   ISBN 0-8101-1483-6
   I. Costlow, Jane T. (Jane Tussey), 1955– II.Title.
   III. Series: European classics (Evanston, Ill.)
   PG3470.Z5T713 1999
   891.73'3—dc21   98-48373
                                    CIP

To Konstantin Andreevich Somov

»»» CONTENTS «««

Translator's Note   *ix*

Introduction   *xi*

The Bear Cubs   3

Zhurya   12

Wolves   20

Deaf Dasha   38

The Monster   61

The Midge   75

The Centaur-Princess   88

The Devil   109

Will   179

»»» TRANSLATOR'S NOTE «««

Lydia Zinovieva-Annibal's prose in *The Tragic Menagerie* combines the descriptive specificity of nineteenth-century realism with an impassioned impulse toward rhythmic cadence and the register of intense emotion. She aims, in this prose, to recapture the world of a child—and a child whose emotional resonance is particular, even acute. Her prose interweaves long, adjective-rich phrases with almost staccato-like passages of dialogue; she occasionally startles with her choice of modifier; there are moments when she steps back and forth from past to present tense, even within the space of a paragraph. All these qualities—and her frequent use of prose that is highly inflected, even musical—are challenges (one is tempted to say adventures!) for a translator. I have tried to honor the particularities of Zinovieva-Annibal's language as much as possible, but doing so (and doing so in a way that will lay claims on the English reader as the Russian does) involves finding appropriate ways to convey the music, the intensity, and the occasional strangeness of her text. I have not adhered with absolute consistency to any one of her modulations (alliteration, say, or shifts in tense), since doing so would have violated what seems to me the larger tenor—the integrity and identity—of her prose. One aims, in the act of translation, for that medial realm that honors, deeply, the original, but which also anticipates the ear of a new reader, or "listener," to whom the voice of Vera (of Lydia Dmitrievna herself) will speak. It is, finally, that voice which I serve. I hope that I have enabled it to sound a bit farther into the world, and to find a response in readers of whom Zinovieva-Annibal herself would not have dreamed.

Finally, I want to acknowledge, and thank, the various readers who have helped me in this work: Marina Shimchenok, Rosa Keselman, and Natasha Tsyganova in Russia; Andrei Strukov, Judith Robbins, and Craig Decker in Maine. David Das, as ever, has contributed wit, wisdom, and great patience.

> I have been amazed, more than once, by a description
> a woman gave me of a world all her own, which she
> had been secretly haunting since her childhood.
> —*Hélène Cixous*

What is childhood—that world we bear within us forever, like a map of promises, some kept, some unfulfilled, a map of possibilities that only we may read? Who is this being to whom we seem only distantly related, whose vivid experience we may treasure or repress? Where is the world that the child so intensely inhabits, contiguous with adults' realities but colored in a palette all its own? It is a country that for many of us holds as much pain as pleasure in remembering, and yet we make the journey, guided either by our own anarchic memories or by the literary signposts of our culture: we travel into childhood with Salinger or Proust, McCullers or Tolstoy, finding in their accounts some resonance with our own fragments of remembrance.

Lydia Zinovieva-Annibal's *Tragic Menagerie* is not a record of childhood with which English-speaking readers will be familiar; first published in Russia in 1907—in the year of its author's death—the work appears here for the first time translated in its entirety. It has, in fact, been largely inaccessible to two generations of Russian readers, for it is only in the years since Russia's *perestroika* that parts of this work have reappeared in Moscow and

Petersburg journals.* The book lay unremembered, languishing in volumes of a symbolist press of the early twentieth century, yet such a brilliant poet as Marina Tsvetaeva, herself a memoirist of childhood, proclaimed it an "enchanting woman's book"; and Maksimilian Voloshin, the poet and critic who had given Tsvetaeva her copy, felt that Zinovieva-Annibal had achieved that rarest of things in her evocation of girlhood: she had summoned up the "metaphysics" of childhood, its genial sense of time, its anguished, turbulent processes of consciousness emerging from the "maternal breast of play." For Voloshin this was a book of confession, of childhood in its own terms, so inaccessible to the adult. It was a book he wanted to share with others as he would share his own intimate joys; he wanted them not only to love it, but to live through it. When Aleksandr Blok, the great Russian symbolist poet, learned of his friend's death, his words pronounced an extremity of loss: "An extraordinary book—*The Tragic Menagerie*, the last book of L. D. Zinovieva-Annibal. . . . We cannot imagine what she might have given Russian literature." But books—like childhood—are never quite lost. And so *The Tragic Menagerie* still haunts us, like that "world all her own" of which Cixous speaks, that world we have been inhabiting in secret since the day we were born.

At the time of its publication, Lydia Dmitrievna Zinovieva-Annibal would have been known to Russian readers (of certain elite circles) as the wife of Vyacheslav Ivanov, Russia's great symbolist poet and philosopher; as the hostess of an important literary salon, held every Wednesday in their Petersburg apartment; and as the author herself of works of prose fiction and criticism. She was a writer of the second rank at best; her work was derivative and mildly scandalous. She seemed so wrapped up in her husband's ideas that

* L. D. Zinov'eva-Annibal, *Tragicheskii zverinets* (Tomsk: Izdatel'stvo Vodolei, 1997).

no one, surely, would have expected anything particularly accomplished from her. But she was, it turned out, a woman of real talent, sorting her way through the fashionable ideas of her time for those words that could be her own. And when she published *The Tragic Menagerie* the critical world took notice: this was a new voice, a new vision, an entry into a created world that was, at last, her own.

Lydia Dmitrievna Zinovieva-Annibal was born in 1866 into a Petersburg family with the highest of connections. On her mother's side she was distantly related to the brilliant poet Aleksandr Pushkin, a connection that her hyphenated last name advertised: "Annibal" was the Abyssinian grandfather of the Russian poet, an exotic connection Pushkin had claimed with pride. The expectations for a daughter in such a family would have been highly conventional, involving a proper education, appearances in society and at court, and a successful marriage. Lydia Dmitrievna, however, seems to have broken the mold at the earliest opportunities: she was educated both at home and in boarding schools (experiences that clearly inform *The Tragic Menagerie*) and tormented a whole series of governesses and teachers. Childhood summers were spent on her family's estate in the Baltic regions of the Russian Empire, a world of intense connections to forest, meadow, and seashore, where a young girl could wander by herself for hours, weaving in and out of imagined identities; a world where bear cubs became playmates and chance encounters with peasant girls led to revelations of larger inequities. Winters, on the other hand, were spent "imprisoned" (a word she herself uses in *The Tragic Menagerie*) by St. Petersburg brick. For the child of *The Tragic Menagerie*, it is the passionate freedom of summer countryside that pulls her spirit; the urban landscape constrains her, drains her of the vibrant energy and emotion we sense in her depictions of the family's estate.

In her late teenage years, Lydia Dmitrievna's parents hired

Konstantin Shvarsalon to tutor their daughter in history. These were years of intense political repression in Russia which nonetheless still resonated with the legacies of idealistic activism so intensely practiced in the 1870s. Throughout that decade Russia had been swept by social movements both altruistic and terrorist; a generation of high-minded, highly educated young men and women went "to the people" in hopes of spreading literacy and a spirit more critical of tsardom. Their less patient contemporaries organized cells of revolutionary activity; in 1881 they had their greatest success—the assassination of the "tsar-liberator" Alexander II. Although this decade of activity was followed by intense political repression, it clearly left in its wake an unquenchable longing for what Zinovieva-Annibal calls, at the end of *The Tragic Menagerie,* "heroic action." When Lydia Dmitrievna met Konstantin Shvarsalon in the early 1880s, he fed her interest in populist socialism with a steady diet of illegal literature. The young woman destined for a brilliant marriage decided, instead, to follow her romantic, populist heart into marriage with Shvarsalon; when her parents resisted, she threatened to enroll in the "Bestuzhev courses" if they did not let her marry. To monarchist parents this was no idle threat, since such courses—instituted as one of the first efforts to provide higher education for women in Russian—were virtually synonymous with radical, immoral behavior. Marriage, however disappointing in social terms, was clearly the preferable course.

As it turned out, Zinovieva-Annibal's parents need not have worried: Shvarsalon proved much less of a zealot than his young wife, quite indifferent after their marriage to the ideals he had championed. Her dowry was perhaps the real reason for his interest; in any case, after the birth of three children and revelations of her husband's affairs, it became clear to Zinovieva-Annibal that the marriage was unsalvageable, and in 1890 she left Russia for Europe with her children. Russian laws made it virtually impossible for a woman to obtain a divorce in such instances. Shvarsalon could have made claims on the children had she returned, so the next few years of Zinovieva–Annibal's life were spent traveling and living in Europe.

The meeting that was to have such a decisive influence on Zinovieva–Annibal's life, her meeting with Vyacheslav Ivanov, took place in 1893 in Rome. Zinovieva–Annibal had been living in Florence and studying music when she was asked by a friend to come to Rome. Ivanov was a classicist and scholar, a man more of books than of lived life; he had made detailed investigations into the ancient cult of Dionysus, intriguing to him for its seeming combination of ecstatic ritualism with the compassionate, suffering ethos of Christ. When Ivanov met Lydia Dmitrievna, he reports, he found the embodiment of Dionysian energy; he found what he had studied in antiquity, embodied in flesh and blood.

Ivanov and Zinovieva–Annibal began their life together in Europe; until her divorce with Shvarsalon was finalized, Lydia Dmitrievna could not risk returning to Russia with her children. In 1899, having received news that a divorce had been granted, Ivanov and Zinovieva–Annibal were married; by this time they had a child of their own, Lydia. When they returned to Russia in the early 1900s, their Petersburg apartment was quickly established as a center of symbolist culture in Russia. Ivanov encouraged Zinovieva–Annibal in her music and writing (she published plays, critical essays, and completed, but never published, a novel), but this work was largely dominated by Ivanov's ideas and the opaque aesthetics of Russian decadence. Zinovieva–Annibal's most public role in these years was as hostess of the couple's salon, where she wore scarlet flowing robes in a stylized Greek fashion, dress that clearly impressed memoirists, who recall her intense, emotional presence.

Ivanov himself suggests that in these years his wife struggled intensely as a creative being, and that she struggled specifically with his influence on her; he seems to have sensed that his own powerful presence was problematic for her as a creative being, that she was still searching for what could be her own way as an artist. The period known in Russian cultural history as the "Silver Age" was a period dominated to a very great extent by feminine imagery; the philosopher Solovyov's theology of "Sophia" (Divine Wisdom) and the poet Blok's mystical imaginings of the "Unknown Woman" are two examples that come quickly to mind. Ivanov's fascination with Dionysus carried with it a mythology of the feminine, embodied in the ecstatic figure of the Meanad, the ritual attendant to Dionysus. The Silver Age enshrined certain myths of femininity—but what did that mean for Russian women who wanted to write, to be creators rather than exemplars of men's myths? One Ivanov scholar has recently suggested that Zinovieva-Annibal parodied symbolist ideas of the feminine in one of her last works, a ribald version of Shakespeare's *Midsummer Night's Dream*. And in her story "Medusa" (published only after her death), Lydia Dmitrievna revisits Blok's famous "Neznakomka" (Unknown Woman), representing Blok himself as part of a sordid, tawdry crew of drunks in a Petersburg tavern. Zinovieva-Annibal seemed to play the part of a decadent, Dionysian woman in literary life, as though the Meanads of her husband's Dionysian imagination had come to life. And yet the last writings of her life suggest a way of freeing herself from roles that had been thrust upon her, a way of beginning to reconnect with a deeper identity. How we understand them—and her—must rest in part on our understanding of the psychology of women's creativity, the complex processes by which all women—not only women artists—move toward autonomy in a world that still defines them primarily according to men's imaginations.

Lydia Zinovieva-Annibal died in the autumn of 1907 from scarlet fever contracted as she ministered to peasants suffering from the disease; *The Tragic Menagerie* was the last work published in her lifetime. It broke quite startlingly with her earlier work and won enthusiastic responses from a broad range of critics. As Voloshin put it, "[Zinovieva-Annibal], who has until now been recherchée, artificial, obscure, and barely comprehensible to the public . . . has in this book found herself at last, has found her own language, simple and expressive, her own style, her own wings."

For late-twentieth-century readers, however, what is most compelling about the work is not its role in the cultural life of prerevolutionary Russia. It is, rather, the startling way this account of girlhood seems to echo with our own memories, to foreshadow some of our own late-twentieth-century dilemmas. Voloshin insists that "only those memories are true about which we have never told anyone." One of the things most compelling and wonderful about *The Tragic Menagerie* is its ability to tell us things we know but of which we have never spoken. The passionate, erotic attachments of girlhood; the soaring emotions of betrayal, longing, disgust; the capacity for empathy and identity with all beings: it is these passions of which the texture of girlhood is woven, Zinovieva-Annibal suggests, and to understand childhood truly we must submit to them again, surrendering ourselves to the turbulent and unpredictable swing of "elemental" nature.

Zinovieva-Annibal called her work "stories," but they are stories that form a deeply connected whole, narrating a journey of self-discovery. Each story bears a revelation of its own; read together their wrenching intensity mounts, as the self we come to know seeks its own freedom, its own way of being in the world. The reader soon comes to realize that the chronology of these tales is not uniform; just as its prose shifts temporality within the space of a page or paragraph, so the sequence of events seems occasionally to backtrack. The mother's illness or the death of a beloved donkey, to which one story refers, seems revoked in a later one, which then narrates a period in the girl's life before the illness or death. What is reliable here, what is important, is less the external chronology than the inner drama, the passage from blessed connections to gradually severed ties; from summer nature to the bitter interiors of a German boarding school; from a mother's caressing presence to the loneliness of an empty attic. This is less the history of childhood than its phenomenology, a narrative of the feeling and language of childhood perception and emotion.

Who are the predominating figures in this landscape of childhood emotion? There is the mother—an intensely felt presence, whose spiritual vision is made explicit in the early chapters of the work but whose love seems gradually attenuated; the animals of Vera's childhood—bears, a crane, wolves, tiny birds, her pet donkeys—beings that link Vera both to the natural world and to herself, and that begin in her the complex process of awakening to difficult moral and psychic truths; and a series of childhood beloveds, almost all women and girls, who are the galvanizing agents of Vera's turbulent, intense emotions. And, of course, there is Vera herself, who is a register for all the sharp turmoil of childhood and its brilliant capacities for connection and imagination. She is what we would call, in American lingo, a tomboy: rambunctious, freewheeling, and determined; able to give as well as get; endlessly stubborn; and possessed of a deep connection to a passionately, physically experienced world—a connection she deeply feels and is determined not to surrender. She becomes a child it might be hard to like—stealing her favorite brother's coins, manipulating schoolroom sweethearts, inking swirls of blood onto penmanship exercises—but she becomes, I think, a girl that many of us will recognize in some deep recess of ourselves. And part of her fundamental importance in the history of childhood is, precisely, this recognition: the "paradise" of childhood we all inhabited is a complicated kingdom. Zinovieva-Annibal's vision is nowhere near as dark as Golding's in *The Lord of the Flies;* yet there is in Vera an impulse to willful destruction, of both herself and others. The deep impulses to love and connection that restrain her are just as anarchic as her will to destruction, and the worlds she inhabits do little to foster those primary forces of compassion. Her final return to the capacities of love is miraculous, unconditional, a gift of both inner and outer natures.

It is, indeed, the nature of Vera's childhood that shapes her most deeply and that seems the most important signature of Zinovieva-Annibal's prose: grounded in the rich summer landscape of Baltic Russia (near enough the sea that she can imagine it vividly from a treetop), Vera's self is embedded to an extraordinary degree in the life of forest, meadow, and sea. She is, literally, an elemental child, a child of earth and water. (One early critic of the work spoke of its "elemental realism.") Her precipitous descent into petty thievery and Godless deceit happens in the imprisoning landscape of cities and institutions—just as "menageries" make mockery of wild beings, so Vera's schoolrooms make mockery of her elemental energies. The dilemmas of human embeddedness in nature—of our animal nature, our relationships to nature and the animal world—are presented in this childhood as those most insistently needful of resolution. Some of the most startling of the book's passages describe Vera's encounters with animals: Vera imagines herself and her dead crane standing before a loving Christ in an apotheosis of nature that will include *all* its creatures; Vera watches the red, bead-sized eyes of a spider, and imagines him watching her ocean-sized spheres; Vera ponders a "monster" brought home from the bog, tormented over whether to intervene in the processes of nature. And Vera names herself as an animal-girl, a centaur-princess—half-human, half-horse—a figure not from ancient mythology but from the fantastic present of a girl who knows she needs only "freedom, and a meadow." Who knows that the prisons of stone—the fathers' houses—must be left behind, in the search for both ground and self.

Finally, it is worth noting the ways in which Zinovieva-Annibal's stories raise issues with which our own ecologically troubled age must struggle. Human intervention in the natural world has few happy outcomes in *The Tragic Menagerie*. Whether describing the rituals of hunting (in her brother's peregrinations and the vicious "tsar's hunt") or Vera's own well-intentioned but abortive acts of compasssion, Zinovieva-Annibal presents as many scenarios of disjunture and destruction as of epiphanic merging. Vera's fascination with "God's creatures" is shadowed by a will to destroy; her compassion is allied to complex, anarchic needs. She is deeply needful of her fields, her forest, her creatures. But she easily, almost knowingly, destroys that which she so deeply loves. How are we to love—Zinovieva-Annibal seems to ask—without destruction? How are we to let nature *be?* How can we live out the Mother's philosophy of compassionate, but dispassionate, caring? The epiphany of contemplative sight with which "The Red Spider" ends suggests some answers and an ecological vision of profound implications. Zinovieva-Annibal does not undertake to unravel just what those implications might be, but in suggesting that the destruction of nature is also a destruction of ourselves, she speaks powerfully to us, children of an environmentally and spiritually ravaged future.

If Zinovieva-Annibal's account of girlhood and self seems so rich to late-twentieth-century readers, there are perhaps good reasons for it: born into a world of extreme privilege; a youngest child who felt increasingly distanced from parental affection; a girl who had the run of a pristine natural world but who encountered early on the nightmarish inequities of her culture; a girl whose vivid emotional life was shaped by an ailing, intense mother; a girl who grew into a budding socialist with a streak of anarchic independence, who retained into adulthood her passion for untrammeled nature; a woman who longed as an adult to find words of her own that might articulate her own vision of woman, body, nature, God. She lived at a time when definitions of God and woman were being tested, when conventions of class and sexuality were being dashed, when harbingers of profound change were already sinking deep into Russian life. That she found a language to tap her aching insights into the primordial tensions of being—lived out intensely in the wild, turbulent passions of a child—is something for which we may be endlessly grateful. By the end of *The Tragic Menagerie* Vera has become a woman, ready to leave her father's house; ready to embark on journeys of love and action; ready to pass on the child of her dead girlhood friend, like a talisman of women's potential to rise from death into a free future. Zinovieva-Annibal's own daughter was named Vera, seventeen years old when the book was published. Did Lydia perhaps write *The Tragic Menagerie* for her daughter— like the mother's note that ends "The Bear Cubs," as words that a girl may set her course by into a bold future? We live in that future, and we bear these promises of childhood in our own worlds of being.

Jane Costlow

»»» SELECT BIBLIOGRAPHY «««

Blok, Aleksandr. "1907: The Literary Year" (Literaturnye itogi 1907 goda), *Sobranie Sochinenii*, vol. 5.

Cixous, Hélène. "The Laugh of the Medusa," in *New French Feminisms: An Anthology*, ed. Elaine Marks and Isabelle de Courtivron (New York, 1981), 246.

Costlow, Jane. "The Gallop, the Wolf, the Caress: Eros and Nature in *The Tragic Menagerie*," *The Russian Review* 56 (April 1997): 192–208.

Davidson, Pamela. "Lydia Zinov'eva-Annibal's *The Singing Ass*: A Woman's View of Men and Eros," in *Gender and Russian Literature*, ed. Rosalind Marsh (Cambridge, 1996), 154–83.

Voloshin, Maksimilan. "Tragicheskii zverinets. Stat'ia o knige Zinov'evoi-Annibal." Unpublished manuscript. Pushkinskii dom, f. 562, op. 1, ed.khr. 206, ll. 1–14.

The Tragic Menagerie

The Bear Cubs

*Dedicated to Margarita Vasilevna Sabashnikova**

My brothers came back from hunting. They had killed a big she-bear. They brought three nurslings with them, tucked into their coats.

It was winter still, and we raised the cubs in our large warm kitchen, on the cellar floor of the wooden house. I remember the first time I saw them. A deep basket of some sort. Someone had tilted it. I looked in. There was a sharp, unpleasant smell. On the bottom of the basket tumbled small, shaggy bodies in straw. That was the funny little bears.

We must have left to spend the rest of winter in town, because the second time I remember the bears they were already moving about; they were beautiful, grown-up bears with fluffy, smooth skin and kind, clean muzzles and cheerful eyes that had a cunning, eager look. There were two of them left: the third had died while still being fed from a bottle.

Our joyful country summer began—mine and my two friends'— the bear cubs.

* Margarita Vasilevna Sabashnikova, wife of Maksimilian Voloshin, herself a gifted painter, did Zinovieva-Annibal's portrait. She was a frequent visitor to the "Tower" (Ivanov and Zinovieva–Annibal's literary salon) in the years before Zinovieva-Annibal's death.

I remember the sun-drenched, sand-strewn courtyard in front of the entry to our large old wooden house; the swing—a long, pliant board on two poles at either end. I sit in the middle of the bowed board, beneath bountiful, fragrant wild roses; with my foot I push quietly, gently off and up, then try to make myself heavy so the swing will bend lower to the ground. The swinging board squeaks beneath me; the bear cubs come out of nowhere, bounding toward me at the familiar squeak, making funny jumps and waddling on their broad, turned-in paws.

They've rushed up big as watchdogs, settle in front of me on the sand and lift their forepaws onto my knees; with one paw each shoved into their gentle jaws, they start in on an extended suck, with much smacking and bellowing.

I remember a passage of classroom dictation: "A hungry bear sucks his paw in winter." But now it's not winter, but summer. And our Mishkas aren't hungry at all, but still they're sucking their broad, brown, tousled paws. Our Mishkas eat oatmeal to their hearts' content. The oatmeal makes them gentle. Now one of them's forgotten me and run off, since he's seen the small dachsund Krotik. Krotik yaps at Mishka. Mishka jumps on Krotik. Krotik is already in Mishka's teeth, but the teeth are softer than the touch of my hands, and the dachsund flies with a delighted yelp out of Mishka's jaws and barks eagerly again, picking at the splendid brown coat of his large, unfettered friend.

I'm jealous. By the paws I pull my second friend, my faithful one. I jump from my board and we chase each other. In no time we're romping in soft, fragrant grass. It smells of spring earth and warm skin, and Mishka's warm breath right in my face makes me laugh with joy, while the flat heavy paws go padding over me. We jump up, run some more. Mishka's on the tree, like a monkey; the heavy paws have grasped the branch tight, and the good, kind, silly head of God's creature hangs downward, shining its cunning, eager eyes at me.

Dear, joyful, sunny spring! God's gift, my forest comrades!

At four o'clock, after lunch on the large semicircular balcony with the white wooden columns, there is tea, coffee and yellow cream, buns with caraway seeds, soft gray bread from our own northern wheat, homemade honey cakes, fizzy drinks, hothouse strawberries and figs and jam to go with them. The whole family gathers: my two older brothers and their former tutor (my younger brother is still with Nurse in the nursery), guests—my brothers' comrades, my sister and her friend, mama, and my governess, the very one who had dictated to me: "In winter the hungry bear sucks his paw."

The honey cakes were delicious! The wife of our old cook was an expert at baking them. They smelled of honey and slightly burned flour. The Mishkas thought so, too. The Mishkas' noses were better at smelling things out than peoples' were. They, of course, were keeping an eye on things here; they would clamber up the side stairs onto the balcony from the big carpet bed, mother's favorite; they stared in at us. People shouted at them; they disappeared and then set us laughing again at the sight of their curious eyes and sniffing nostrils.

But the young people, with their lack of good sense, went blithely off about their own business once they'd finished the feast—and the Mishkas, who had waited for their time to come, were already on the table.

"Oh no, the honey cakes!" mother remembered. She runs, I'm right after her. The big Mishkas have clambered awkwardly into the middle of the round family table. They're gobbling up honey cakes. They've overturned the jam. They're sucking on their sweet paws. They smack their lips and snort. Their little eyes dart cunningly about.

They've noticed us. Started rushing about. The heavy table wobbles; glasses and plates poured off in all directions.

The Mishkas go smack on the floor, and only their fat rear ends with the short fluffy tails were swaying as they bolted down the stairs. Mama wasn't upset.

Mama was gentle, and loved the silly Mishkas.

Summer progressed. The bears grew not by the day but by the hour. They grew bigger by far than the average watchdog. They played with the dachshund as in the past, romped with me as before, and, as was their unchanging habit, kept an eye out for sweet things left unguarded, but still gobbled up their oatmeal, bellowing gratefully.

But our harmless friends were beginning to inspire misgivings in peasants who came to the estate. Bears raised by landowners seemed a bad business to them—and they looked at them askance, warily, and avoided them out of fear. Then I heard that the elder had come to complain to my brother; he asked us to take the bears away.

"Out of nowhere they'll attack somebody, tear them up. Or the livestock, too . . . Still and all it's a forest creature, never mind it was raised on a bottle."

The bears were taken off to the brick shed. The gates were kept locked. The Mishkas howled mournfully, begged to be let go, to the sunshine, to their friends . . . I walked about like a lost soul, got into trouble, was mean to my governess, wept . . .

A meeting of the family and the forest warden was called, to decide the bear cubs' final fate. We were headed into the second half of summer. By autumn the cubs will be full-grown bears. You mustn't set them free now. And there's no point keeping them locked in the shed. You have to feed them meat already.

"Shoot them?" suggested the forest warden.

From the corner of the large old sofa, where I'd taken refuge, unnoticed, I started to wail. My older brother wavered.

"It's reasonable . . . Of course, it's reasonable . . . And it's possible to do it painlessly . . ."

My second brother, The Wild Hunter—as family members called him for his love of solitary forest adventures—didn't agree . . .

"We've gotten used to them, we raised them. We nursed them. You won't lift a finger against them!"

I emitted broken howls as I listened. Sister got teary:

"Mama dearest, think of something!"

"Let them out in the forest!" said mother.

I stopped my loud howling and shut my mouth. Everyone was quiet. My older brother shrugged his shoulders. The forest warden objected:

"Still and all, it's awkward. Still and all, the animal's wild. Tears the cows apart."

I hated him. My Mishkas were not "wild animals."

"It is awkward," seconded my older brother, but without conviction.

Sister looked at Mother with moist pleading eyes. I got ready to howl. Had already opened my mouth. But the Wild Hunter said quick-temperedly:

"Mama's right. That's what needs to be done. Take them out to the forest. We have no right to shoot the bears."

And Mother added quickly:

"We took them from the forest. If we hadn't, they'd have still been running around there now."

My older brother wanted to agree, and agreed. The forest warden was won over, and everyone started discussing how to set the Mishkas free. This is what we decided: to put them in large, bolted crates and cart them into the forest beyond Devil's Bog. It's far away and wild. Deposit the crates in the forest, knock out the nails, and head out quickly. By the time the Mishkas have figured out the boards, the cart will already be far away. They wouldn't find the road in a million years. And there, at liberty in a slumbering forest of pine, they will grow wild . . .

The Wild Hunter laughed:

"Then they'd better watch out for me. We won't recognize each other. I'll shoot!"

We carted them out.

The minute their fate was decided was so dreadful, and the hope, after despairing for their freedom and life, so joyfully acute, that I forgot to miss my transported comrades. It wasn't the time for it now. Something fearful had passed my soul by, and my soul tucked inward.

I don't know how many days passed. Maybe only one or two, no more, and I learned the horrible, final news. I don't remember how I found out, where, with what words. All words merged into one— a feeling, really, not a word—since I was able to give it a name, to mark it with a word, only much later. Betrayal. Someone had betrayed someone. A kind of joyous, childlike love—no, simpler than that, an animal trust—was betrayed . . . betrayed.

Beyond Devil's Bog the peasants and women folk were mowing in a forest meadow. Suddenly they saw two bears running straight toward them from the wood. Out of fear they took them for grown bears. The peasants and women folk took fright and met the bear cubs with scythes . . .

The bear cubs ran lovingly toward humans, toward the kind voices of friends, their cunning eyes gay and eager; their broad rear ends waddling funnily on their powerful, turned-in paws. *That* was how I saw them.

The frightened peasants met the bears with scythes. They hacked at them. One of them they caught alive. They took him to the tsar's park to sell for the royal hunt. They'll break his paws before the hunt so it'll be easier to shoot, and less dangerous. The other one, covered with wounds and slash-marks, all bloody, not understanding a thing, somehow broke loose; startled, he headed back into the woods.

My Wild Hunter brother was riding horseback with a gun over his shoulder, lost in thought, as he loved to be. He heard someone groaning. Like a human . . . following the groan, he made his way into the grove. Our own Mishka lay there, dying. He was still able to see my brother. My brother lowered his gun from his shoulder and drained all his shot into the bear's ear.

That's how our Mishkas ended their lives.

I remember and know that it happened that way, but who told me and where, I don't remember, nor does it matter. No doubt, the Wild Hunter told me. What I remember is my mother's face, probably when my brother was talking about the bear cubs' death. Since then, that is the face of Mother's I remember most clearly. So pale, and the full lower lip jumping strangely. And in her eyes—so bright and large—was fear. And then she stood up and staggered. I jumped up. Brother also came running. Her lip trembling, she said quietly then, apologizing:

"It's nothing, Mitya. I felt a bit sorry for our Mishkas. I'll be right back."

And she went out . . . It grew very quiet. Probably everyone went out. But suddenly I heard something that I remembered, absurdly, word for word, though its meaning was still unclear to me then. The chastening voice of my brothers' old tutor seemed quite near me as he uttered the words:

"That is where it all leads, when man meddles with the life of nature."

And the sober-minded governess answered him:

"But what, would you order that wild animals not be destroyed and have them kill the peasants' livestock?"

I wanted to cry. Understood nothing. Wanted to cry, but couldn't.

I remember—it's already dark. I'm already in the nursery, in bed, not sleeping, and still tears don't come. The weather vane squeaks its quiet iron squeak on the roof. An unbearable weight has descended on my heart. Evil has been done. A great injustice. Trust and love have been betrayed. A betrayal. A betrayal of love and trust. And . . . no one is to blame.

No one is to blame. At night, in the darkness, beneath the iron creak of the weather vane, the thought came clearer, almost in words. I couldn't cry. The unspoken question weighed terribly on my heart. Its weight was too much for my heart.

I crawled out of bed. I felt with my hands before me in the dark. I made my way down the long corridor to Mother.

Mother will say. Mother will answer. Mother, Mother . . . Mama has to know everything. Mama can save you from everything.

"Mama, Mama! Why did God permit it?"

"Little one, there is no justice on earth! There cannot be . . . But you love the earth, wish it justice, pray for justice, burn in your heart, my child, for justice, and a miracle must happen. It will come to be, the world of justice. That which the soul wants so very much comes to be."

"Mama, you said on earth there couldn't be . . ."

"A miracle, my child, a miracle. A gift from heaven. But it's not worth living for this earth. It's worth living for heaven's gift, my child, only for that gift. Worth suffering and crying. And burning and praying."

"But living, Mama, how can you live when you're sad?"

"Live? . . . Listen, my child, this is how: you must love. That's how you must live. I don't know anything else. Love will teach you. Love is demanding. The larger and more holy your love is, the more demanding it is. Demanding love will teach you not to forgive injustice. Your hand will grow firm, and your heart strong . . . Grow further than I, understand more . . . *Great be thy love, and more shalt thou demand.*"

I knelt on the small rug by her bed, my face sunk into her hands, and suddenly the tears came, flowing into my mother's kind hands . . .

It grew easier . . . Then I felt like sleeping.

She didn't let me go alone, back through the long, dark corridor to the nursery. She tucked me in beside her. It was warm and tender. There was certainty and salvation in that tender maternal warmth. And I fell asleep that way . . .

Mother died when I was still a young child. I wouldn't have remembered her words so clearly. But after her death a dark blue envelope remained, with an inscription in her hand: "To Verochka, when she turns sixteen." In the envelope, marked with the date when my brother had shot the tormented bear cub, lay a letter—not even a letter, just a note. That night Mother wrote down our conversation, that I might remember it all my life.

»)») «(«(«

Zhurya

*Dedicated to Olga Aleksandrovna Beliaevskaia**

I had a baby crane named Zhurya. In the spring my dear Wild Hunter brother pulled him out of his hunter's bag and handed him over to me. For two days and two nights he had wandered in the woods, with his two pointers; he brought home two bags of dead birds, with heads that dangled on withered, flabby necks; five rabbits with lifeless, dark, lusterless little eyes; and then a third bag— from which he pulled Zhurya, alive, and gave him to me in the corridor. Zhurya was still an ungainly featherless fledgling on long awkward legs, with a small sharp-eyed head high on his crane's neck.

At first Zhurya grew in the light-filled storeroom in our house, where the canaries lived; then later, when it was already summer, when he'd grown to be slender and strong and was covered with smooth ash-gray feathers, I took him out into the apple orchard.

The orchard was fenced off from the park with a high paling. One of Zhurya's wings worked badly, and his feathers had been shaved off on both wings as well, so he couldn't fly away. That's where he lived, feeding on fabulous worms in the fat rows of raspberries and

* Olga Aleksandrovna Beliaevskaia, a poet and prose writer primarily for children, published in *The Path*, a journal for children edited by Poliksena Solovyova. She was a frequent visitor to the salon hosted by Zinovieva-Annibal and Ivanov at the Tower in Petersburg.

on caterpillars. That was where he and I spent the happy hours of our friendship. How lively he was, such a mischief maker!

We would walk out of the orchard beyond the paling, through the whole park. I run along the paths; Zhurya flaps his wings and flies along in bursts among the trees. I lie down in the grass, and Zhurya tweaks me on the dress, tears painfully at my hair, and babbles something incomprehensible and wheezing.

Zhurya is my fine-feathered dog, my easygoing, free-spirited friend, my pride. I walk and smile.

"What are you thinking about?" asks my governess. "About your Zhurya, probably."

Once Zhurya wasn't in the apple orchard. I called and called, yelled till I was hoarse, tore up my knees on the gooseberry bushes, and cried. My heart sank into some deep, painful place, pinched itself into a ball.

The day passed gray, lonely, hopeless. I was bad-tempered and stubborn. At night I cried, didn't sleep . . . I plucked up considerable courage: I got quietly up, slipped out the window (my room was on the second floor), made my way along the trellis slats onto the nearby roof of the large balcony, and slipped down its moonlit-white column into the orchard.

In the orchard I feared nothing—though I'd thought that I would. And there in the orchard, under apple trees long since stripped of blossoms, among rows unfamiliar in the shadows of moonlight, so severe and unmoving, so distinct and abrupt—I ran, searched, called, and cried.

In the evening of the next day they brought Zhurya back alive—alive, but pecked all over, with a broken wing. The cranes had done it. Other ones, wild ones, there in the fields where the oats were ripening. Zhurya had flown toward them there. They didn't understand their little brother, didn't take the stranger's hand, and beat him with their beaks. Toward evening, Wild Hunter was riding home from the woods on Orlik and decided to shoot the greedy cranes in the oats. Cranes are crafty: without a gun they'll let you come close, but if they see a gun they'll take off with a squeaky whoop from half a verst away.* They took off, but one flew a bit and fell with a thud. My brother made his way along the row of oats—it was Zhurya!

They locked Zhurya up in the greenhouse. It was boring for him there among the tame rows of coddled plants; there were no fat worms and caterpillars in the pots, no leaping of frogs after rain on the dull, leveled walkways.

But I came for him every day. He rushed toward me with a squeaky greeting, and we went out into freedom. He grew stubborn and strong.

We would walk toward the stables. But he didn't like that path, between the meadow and the dried-up pond. He had his own foolish notions! What was there not to like? I didn't understand. I shove the stubborn thing forward, pressing with the force of my eight-year-old hands on his tall, flat, resistant back on long, strong legs. I shove. We run three steps forward, five steps back.

I'm all sweaty, quite peevish from my efforts, angry and laughing at my stubborn, strong friend.

In the stable yard, along the shed overhang, planks are laid out on ground brown and glistening with manure, sharp smelling and pungent; alongside them and beneath the overhang is a gutter for the watery manure; it's deep and swampy there beneath the metallic rainbow-colored film of mold.

It's awful.

We make our way shoving and struggling along the narrow boards. We press up close against the fence. That board is a bit shorter. I bend over. I'm working at it. I've turned it over. Zhurya

*A *verst* is a prerevolutionary unit of measure, roughly equivalent to two-thirds mile.—Trans.

stood angry and silent. Suddenly, what a cackle, at the top of his voice. Worms! Worms! Oh, what amazing worms! Rose ones. No, they're so fat they're even yellow, like the salmon you get during Lent. They lie on the dungy ground, barely moving. Zhurya swallows them one after another, with a burbling of fat. What a feast! What a feast! Too bad I can't have some! Oh well, it doesn't matter: I understand how good it must taste, how awfully good.

The autumn was long, boring. It got inconvenient to go for walks with Zhurya, and then . . . I'd gotten a bit tired of it. I'd grown used to him, my heart no longer pined for my friend, alone there now in the distant, unheated greenhouse.

There are pots with earth there: there are probably worms even there. There are tubs with water, too, dug into the ground: why shouldn't there be frogs as well? I think: of course there are.

Anyway, I take Zhurya barley. He loves grain. Happy to see me. Wants to be let out. But often I have no time! There are lessons, of course: in autumn there are more lessons, the governess is stricter, I'm lazier, more stubborn, and I'm often rude and often punished. Then there's no time for Zhurya. At least nobody punishes Zhurya. I envy him. I'd be happy to be with him, but of course how could I, every day? In the spring, now—that's when we'll be friends again.

For three days I didn't go to Zhurya. I went and took some grain and poured water into his container; the most important thing is water, because the greenhouse tubs are deep, and, though they're dug level with the ground, they're often ladled half-empty after watering, and they're narrow: if Zhurya fell in, he couldn't use his wings to get out . . .

For four days I didn't go. I remembered. Took the grain.

Then I got into big trouble. I had run out to Maria in the field, hauled potatoes all day long with her, stood on the cart and drove the horse. I came back in the evening all covered in autumn mud, with one of my shoes lost in the field. I was sent to my room for two days. I turned malicious. Hard-hearted. Forgetful.

A week went by. I'm sitting doing lessons, forgiven but not resigned. Across from me sits Elena Prokhorovna—my pale, tormented governess, exhausted body and soul by me. Suddenly . . . Zhurya! Zhurya has no grain! Zhurya has no water!

I tear from my seat without asking, speed along the corridor, barrel down the stairs, another corridor and another stairway, this one already dark, the stone one into the cellar where our large kitchen is. The dishwasher brings me a pot of barley and pours boiling water over it. Zhurya loves it that way. I run for the wagon. The pot is on the wagon. Elena Prokhorovna calls from the porch; I race past without answering, down the path to the greenhouse.

I'm smiling ear to ear. He's starved. But today there's his favorite grain, with boiled water. And hunger will make it so tasty! And I'll never, never forget again. Today my heart overflows with love, it's even heavy in my chest, it's even hard to run with such a full heart. I want to stop and start crying, and whisper loudly: "I love you! I love you! Forgive me! I'll never forget! I love you! I love you, oh I love you! . . ."

It's quiet and empty in the greenhouse. Unpleasantly quiet.

"Zhurya! Zhurya!"

It's quiet. Oh, a quiet that bodes no good!

"Zhurya! Zhurya!"

I run all over. The gardener didn't take him, did he? He hadn't died of hunger? Because there aren't any worms in the disgusting clean pots. And it's not true that frogs can wander about on these skyless, rainless walkways.

I run back toward the door. At the door stands a tub, dug into the ground. There's something gray in the deep tub, a long neck floats up out of the depth, unmoving in the water, withered and flabby; someone's lifeless eye, dark and lusterless, comes from the depths to meet my eyes, approaching it . . . I scream. I scream. I haven't the strength to go closer. I know it's all over.

I run to the gardener. I scream. I scream.

The gardener is with me by the tub. He pulls out Zhurya.

"He wanted a drink. What, Verochka, did you forget to bring him water? He drowned a long time ago. See how he's gone stiff."

I can't look. I can't speak. Despair creeps in on me from somewhere; I sense it and scream. I muffle the despair with a wild cry and shuffle slowly up the walkway toward the house, wailing and wailing, not closing my mouth. Mother comes to meet me, and the governess, and sister, and the housekeeper, my brother, and my other brother, too.

But I wail without hope, without letting up, someone has clamped my heart with pincers, has clenched it into a ball, and burning blood flows, flows, flows, flows . . .

Late. Late. Late . . .

So the winter passed. By then we were in town. Was it forgotten? It would drop out of memory and then be recollected. I prayed badly that winter. The sin could not be atoned for, and I was unable to beg forgiveness for it from God.

A new spring began. We went to the country for Passion Week and Holy Week.

I fasted for the first time. Quiet and devout I went to church, where before I had been lazy and got tired. I knelt and prayed for hours, crying. I was meek, mild.

On the evening of Good Friday I went to confession. I trembled, a faint, quiet trembling, as I passed through the dark church toward the choir, where the old priest waited for those who came to confession. I stood with lowered head. To everything I answered, "I have sinned, Father!" Then when he asked if there wasn't something in particular, I told him about Zhurya, how I had drowned Zhurya because I'd grown tired of loving him. I was silent, waiting . . . Would he forgive me? And could one forgive me at all? Impossible, impossible; oh, of course it was impossible. I was damned, because I'd grown tired of loving . . .

And bitter, sparse tears began to fall . . .

"Verochka, don't cry anymore. Man is weak in his love. How can it be otherwise? It is Christ who loves. It is Christ, our God, who forgives. He will forgive you, too. He came to accomplish his task, unto the end. We humans are incapable of that. But we can pray and ask for help. For if He forgives and is merciful—He will take your soul and give you life again. Then the soul will learn to love. It is He who can do all things, because He died and was resurrected."

And the old priest bade me kneel, covered my head with his rustling, incense-fragrant stole, and whispered something. A chill ran along my spine, the tears stopped. There was such quiet that all my thoughts fled, and trust alone remained.

Now it is Easter Eve. The snow is melting. It drips from the roofs. A rustling, a swelling, a whispering of all the earth, a dialogue in whispers with the sky, where warm breath wafts from the lofty, fiery stars . . .

The sleigh slides along sunken, thawed snow without squeaking. On thawed patches it shudders with the touch of iron on still slippery earth. Quiet. It smells of pine pitch spring. And each tree, still black and sparse, distinct in the bright starry steam, is a vial of incredible, magical fragrances . . .

The village is filled with movement. Something is happening. Something is happening. The stars know it, and the wind, and the earth, and the people.

I am clean: I washed, my hair as well, until it was squeaky clean; I even wiped my teeth with lemon so they'd be white. My dress is white, too. And I'm silent, silent. Since Friday evening I have counted the words, so my soul would stay white after absolution and Holy Communion.

It is light, and the light of candles flickers, flowing back and forth. People sigh quietly, cross themselves, and bow, their faces hot and bright as they wait, expectantly . . . then the heedful, quiet crowd parts; the priest and deacon pass through, and the choristers with banners and crosses . . . The crowd surges after the procession. Air pours in from the courtyard; in the incense and in the wax is the smell of unimaginable birches.

"Christ is risen! Christ is risen! Christ is risen!"

And three times the fervent answer:

"In truth He has risen!"

In truth, of course! My heart has risen in my breast. My weak heart, so unable to love, has risen, in order to give of itself. And it gives itself up to you, my Christ and my God!

And life and death become strangely one in my childish breast. It only seems that they are different. Nothing is dreadful for this heart reborn in love, and nothing is painful, neither for me nor for others.

You live, my dear Zhurya! I didn't love you? How could it be . . . if you want I'll die for you, right now, here, so you can be alive, beside me.

You live, Zhurenka, you are with Christ. We will meet there. Have you forgiven your silly, weak, forgetful friend? She is different. Today, right now, she is different. She is stronger than death. Stronger than life. Today she is whole, and you today are whole. That is Christ.

Is that what I *thought* then? That is what I *remember* now.

So when the tarnished earth is transformed, the ailing earth, the flickering earth, transformed from death into life, the earth that begs to stop but rushes on, rushes in its crushing whirlwind (that is how I, too, was then, as in a whirlwind)—when it is transformed, there will be eternal Easter, and you, my silly, dear Zhurya, will stand whole with me before Christ, and then you and I both will look into the eyes of forgiveness.

»»» 《《《

Wolves

*Dedicated to Maksimilian Voloshin**

It was late autumn. My brothers and sister had long since left for town to study and dance. My aunt had settled in with them in our apartment there, to escort my sister and look after the house, since Mama was sick. Mama's legs hurt, and she couldn't walk. The doctor was urging her south, to go about in her wheelchair in the sun, but she wanted to stay longer in the country, where she would willingly have spent the whole winter in the large, warm, old house.

In late autumn the tsar's hunt came to our village. Lots of packs of hounds, borzois, lots of riders, the leader of the hunt himself, a severe German of few words, and with him a kind of guest-devotee, a handsome, dapper gentleman with whom I fell in love—Vladimir Nikolaevich.

In the village that evening long troughs of some kind were filled with bloody viscera (I found out that the hunt had bought up peasants' old horses) and chunks of raw horse flesh. Then they let the high-strung, hungry dogs up to the troughs, trembling and wriggling. The dogs, snarling and yelping, pounced on the viscera; the huntsmen

* Maksimilian Voloshin (1877–1932), an artist, a poet, a critic, and a translator from the French, was acquainted with, but largely independent of, the symbolists. His unpublished essay on *The Tragic Menagerie* offered high praise for this "confession" of childhood.

stood beside the troughs with long whips and lashed to right and left, warding off fights . . .

The leader of the tsar's hunt and Vladimir Nikolaevich stayed with us in the main house. I fell in love with the marvelous, clean-shaven Vladimir Nikolaevich over dinner, as he recounted, for my English governess, Miss Florry, after the early departure of the close-mouthed German leader, how the tsar's hunt catches wolves alive.

The huntsmen cordon off one part of the forest with high, strong nets; in all other directions local peasants, called in by the hundreds, are closely interspersed. The peasants are armed with clubs and rakes, and yell loudly, their yells keeping the wolves from getting by them out of the forest. Huntsmen on horseback make their way into the woods with packs of hounds. The hounds smell out the wolf and pursue him toward the net with their high-pitched barking; the wolf hits it at a run, then a second net falls from above; he thrashes and gets so tangled there's no getting out. The huntsmen arrive. They bend the animal's neck to the ground with a two-pronged clamp; they tie his legs like a sheep's; once they've turned him on his back, they put a thick, short stick crossways into his open mouth, and when it's tightened with a rope at the withers, they lift the animal by its bound legs onto a thick pole. Once they've hoisted the pole onto their shoulders, two men carry the wolf face upward onto the main road, where huge covered wagons, like freight cars, await the captives.

"Where do they take them?" Miss Florry sternly asked Vladimir Nikolaevich; he liked her stern demeanor and was teasing her.

"Oh, Heavens, to the tsar's park for the tsar's hunt."

"Why hunt wolves that have already been caught?"

"For amusement. You see, they break one leg on each of them, so they won't run away too fast . . . and also so they can't attack."

"How disgusting! It's fine that you're concerned for public welfare, carting off wolves. But why this barbarian cruelty?"

It's approximately thus I remember the conversations between Vladimir Nikolaevich and Miss Florry from that still-early childhood, and I fell in love with him—of course, not for myself, but for my older sister who had gone to town. Then, too, Vladimir Nikolaevich talked a great deal about himself, about how he'd performed brilliantly on some sort of exams that he hadn't prepared for at all, and how impudently he had answered everyone; and as he talked he smacked his full, beautifully sculpted lips, and I envied him and was enthralled by him—thinking of my sister.

On the evening the tsar's hunt arrived, after my usual evening prayers by her bed, Mama said to me:

"Verochka, tomorrow at dawn Fedor will harness the big wagons; several ladies—the teacher, the village medic, and others, even our Emma Yakovlevna (that was our housekeeper) would like to meet the hunt in the Kerbokov forest and see how they catch live wolves. If you want, I'll let you go with Miss Florry."

Of course I wanted to. I turned Mama's slender white hands palms upward; I kissed them, and her marvelous blue eyes with their big whites, with frenetic emotion.

From excitement I got virtually no sleep and was in the stables too early.

The stable boy was leading horses from the stable into the carriage shed, where two smudge lamps still burned in the predawn darkness. Krasavchik neighed and stamped with his foreleg, tangling the trace. Fedor yelled out in his high-pitched tenor:

"Monkey around, will you! Your leg!" and he hit Krasavchik with his fist on the leg, freeing the trace from under his hoof.

I echoed in a wheezy bass:

"Your leg!" and got in Fedor's way, fearlessly hitting Krasavchik in the leg after he did.

The bay Krasavchik gave a high-pitched, joyful neigh, and tossing his head onto the imperturbable, dark-ginger Malchik's neck, bit and scraped him in the withers with his broad, blunt yellow teeth. There was tramping on the wooden floor of the shed, the bustling and cursing of coachmen, the smell of leather, manure, and horse sweat; the autumn morning chill blew in, bringing a sharp scent of rotting leaves and rye from the nearby barns. It was the smell of autumn, my favorite, vigorous and urgent.

Fedor the coachman went to get dressed. I shoved Malchik's tail under the breechband and feared nothing, feeling myself twice as alive for that fearlessness . . . Then I bridled Krasavchik, who clicked his teeth and sprayed spume as he shook his smooth muzzle, and I intoned "monkey around" in a deep voice, bit my teeth, and knit my brows with preoccupied intensity.

Fedor, an upright, handsome man with shining black hair, stern penetrating eyes, and a narrow, dark, serious face (in summers Fedor was for me the most powerful and most adored being on the estate), came back in a dark blue kaftan-vest over a red shirt, and was quickly on the coach box, with me on the broad wagon bed, which hung across long, strong crossbeams. In the wagon bed there were three places on a back bench, three on one in front, and three on one that ran lengthwise. Broad flat running boards in back, and running boards in front.

The horses moved along the alley toward the house entranceway.

Miss Florry and Emma Yakovlevna got in, I hopped onto the back running board, and we set off for the village to gather the "village aristocracy" who wanted to observe the tsar's hunt for wolves.

The fields were pale with dawn. Near the large hay barn, where, amid the crisp autumn bustle, there was the oddly belated, honeyed fragrance of haying in June, we caught up with the hunt and set off at a trot. Through the distinct clatter of mounted horses on a road cold and hard with autumn's morning frost, through the glassy crunch of newly formed ice, shattered by their ringing shoes, I heard the unfamiliar rustling scratch of dogs' paws by the dozen.

The long lashes snapped and slapped mercilessly along the dogs' lithe spines; the dogs cowered beneath the blows; the riders' cries carried far in the empty transparent air of the fields. The dogs were tied in pairs, and the pack coiled dark and glossy, a many-bodied, many-headed serpent, moving quickly along the icy gray road between two rows of horses.

Vladimir Nikolaevich pranced along beside us, annoying his dappled gray horse with the reins and teasing the ladies from our "aristocracy."

"It does happen that the wolves tear through the nets, and then, mind yourself and be quick!"

The teacher with her knee-length braid, whom I worshiped for her feminine charm; the daughter of our estate manager, short-haired, with an African mouth and penetrating gray eyes, whom I feared and loved with a piercing, hidden love; the priest's daughter, red-haired, malicious and a toady, whose father—our cheerful, widowed old priest—said of her in the most incomprehensible way, that "piligrims" had been coming to call for five years, but no one took her; and the manly village medic—all these young women and the old women, too, the one who worked at the post office and the one who baked communion bread, all listened to Vladimir Nikolaevich and were afraid.

"Especially if it's a full-grown wolf, he's quite strong and dreadfully malicious . . ."

Often I would hop down from the back running board, race by those who were seated, and clamber onto the one toward the front, beside Fedor. Both running boards above the low wheels made two convenient, though jolting, platforms for my gymnastics.

"Fedor, give Krasavchik a whip, the right trace is wandering there."

"That's when we're headed uphill, Verochka. Can't you see? He's really working at it. Malchik's the one who's crafty, but he's a no-foolin' harse!" (It was funny to me how Fedor called a horse a "harse." That was because Fedor had come from the foundling home and had been educated by Karelians. That's what I heard my brother explain to a friend. And he'd added, quite incomprehensibly, "He may even be a prince. That's where his fine features are from.")

It already smelled more strongly of pine needles and the bog. The fields had ended; all around stood forest. Even here, still in complete shadow, you suddenly sensed that somewhere beyond the distant field the sun had risen. A chill, distant light suddenly tinted the treetops amber. The tops of the birches shook fiercely in the wind, their bare branches twining in among one another. The pines were dark and boring, the firs green and elegant; on the brown earth lay yellow, red, gray, purple leaves, covered in hoarfrost . . . A hut! You could build a hut! There's more brushwood there than you can get through . . .

The horses set off at a walk . . . then they stopped. The huntsmen crowded about the dogs, in a hurry. Once freed, the dogs soon tore away from the thick of it, shaking themselves and yelping. Cries, bustle, barking, lashes . . . then everything quiet again. The huntsmen and dogs disappeared into the wood. We're alone on the road.

I go have a look at the wagon with the large metal cages for the wolves. Then I go up closer to the high wall of bare birches and black pine trees covered with nets.

I wander quietly away from the people I've come with, clustered timidly about the wagon. In the forest I'm bored with people. In the forest I like being alone.

And quickly my imagination carries me off, away from this tame and well-ordered life, into another one, wild, free, nomadic . . . I'm the princess of a nomad camp . . . I'm on a hunt. I must feed my people; but today the enemy surrounded our encampment, they want to catch us and eat us. The enemy are ogres. I'm alone, alone I've crept out of the hut, and now I make my way fearlessly through the bushes, looking for a way out, for a way to save us, some way to lead my people secretly into open forest and escape the enemy . . . But the wolves . . . All the wolves in the forest have turned rabid . . . What can be more terrible than a rabid wolf? He fears no one, throws himself at a crowd, and bites now one and then another . . . and they turn rabid, too . . . you have to tie them up . . . It's the enemy who has infected the wolves with rabies, so they'll destroy my people, but we've hung nets on the trees to protect ourselves from the wolves, and now I'm keeping watch while all my people sleep . . .

What a smell of mushrooms! Aha—a death cap! It's no good, you can't eat it. But what a beauty, how splendid and scarlet! And those little white stars on the royal purple . . . And it's not as though he's bad: he keeps watch over the captured pine mushrooms. The death cap is a terrible guard! He spurts poison at anyone who dares come close to the pine mushrooms. They're princes under a spell, and the death cap is a fiery dragon. There they are! Oh how wonderful! A family: the father, the mother, and seven, eight, nine, eleven children. Where's the twelfth? There are always twelve sons, if you only have boys. How very, very strong they are! Dark brown as oak leaves in autumn, glistening and pungent. How cold and cheery they are when I lay them against my frozen nose. Oh, barking! It's the enemies. They're after me with dogs . . . I run . . . and run . . . But the pine mushrooms! It's shameful to drop my loot. Better to die. Otherwise my people will die of hunger.

Wolves! Wolves! The tsar's hunt. The high-pitched, unhurried barking continues en masse, without break, increasing as it comes closer. Already I can make out separate voices: one drawls deeper, the other sharper. And there are wild howls. My heart has stopped. Who is howling? Oh, it's not a game anymore. These are really and truly wolves! Who are they slashing? Who has set to howling so wildly? Many, many voices. It's peasants chasing the wolves back into the forest. Then there's a pounding of horses and branches breaking, like fire crackling and hissing through the woods.

Barking—barking—barking!

"Vera—Vera—Vera!"

Miss Florry's dear voice! I tear toward her, hands stretched before me and mouth open wide, howling like a wolf in horror at being pursued . . .

Suddenly the dogs grow quiet. I sit in the wagon with the "village aristocracy" and feel embarrassed . . . Not one of them is scared. They're laughing. I'm embarrassed and don't answer their questions, I'm rude, ill-tempered, contemptuous.

They're bringing it. Two people are already bringing it along. It's him. It's the terrible wolf. Maybe it's rabid? The aristocracy presses into a tighter knot, almost all of them are sitting together on one lengthwise seat. They carry him by us upside down. His head hangs toward the road. All four legs are tied together, and a thick club runs through the rope. The huntsmen's shoulders bend. A full-grown wolf is heavy. There come some more, and still more . . . Then somewhere in the distance the glassy barking drawls out again, at first like the drone of a mosquito in your ear. They've taken the dogs into the forest again. Or is it the second pack?

Vladimir Nikolaevich rides up to the cages.

"It's not dangerous. They're all tied up! And I'm here with you!"

Of course, nothing and no one is dangerous with him!

We go over.

I look at the wolves through the thick bars in the grille. The whole floor is covered. Five of them . . . yes, five. They lie like rams with legs bound tightly together. The ropes 'round their necks that hold the stick in their mouths are cut now, but their teeth still clench and lunge at the wood with wild obstinacy. They don't let go of the wooden bits.

I feel sorry for the wolves. That repulsive, slippery, flabby feeling comes creeping into my chest. I shove it away: wolves are evil, they eat sheep, they ate my donkey, Mama's old Golubchik that she rode when she was a little girl . . . Wolves are evil and disgusting cowards! They attack loners in packs . . . What nasty eyes!

"There's a disgusting face!" says Vladimir Nikolaevich.

Of course it's disgusting! Vladimir Nikolaevich is always right. The little eyes watch with evil horror, like little coals—of course, like searing little coals! At night they glow like little green lanterns, wolf eyes do.

Horrible, horrible! They've opened the cage door; they've dumped one more in and shoved him deeper.

"Oh, how nasty!" exclaims the village medic. "He has a wound in his side. Why didn't they kill him? It's better for an animal than a human—you can kill him."

I look at her tall, manly figure. I want to be a doctor.

"We're not supposed to, ma'am. We're ordered to get them alive!" the panting huntsman explains to her.

"Poor animal!" Miss Florry murmurs in English, and moves away from the cage with a fastidious face.

"What a stinking cage!" says Emma Yakovlevna.

"What repulsive beasts!"

And the rest of the ladies walk away.

"It's dreadfully interesting!"

The dogs are near again. Another party will be here soon.

"Time to go home!" calls Miss Florry. "I don't care for this kind of hunt. If it were on horseback with a gun, I myself would shoot. But this way—it's unpleasant, pathetic!"

But I've had a good look, and I've long since been crying. This wolf has been poked through the side with a rake. He breathes through a hole in his side. The air hisses, and it seems as though I hear it through the hole; the edges of his wound move up and down. It's horrible. The wolf's teeth have bit the stick in his mouth;

quite close to my face, where it's pressed against the bars, are his eyes. In their corners I see the white part. It's all bloody. His pupils strain straight into my pupils. Unbearable pain, furious hatred, and sorrow are condensed in them, along with a final, hopeless, settled horror. These pupils have laid a spell on me and I, like him, clench my bared teeth and drill my wild pupils, dried now of their recent tears. I hear my grimace. The skin stretches dry. With my ears I hear my repellant wolf face, the hatred, horror, and pain in its pupils and in its stretched-out lips . . . The air keeps hissing as it bursts from the bloody hole in the side, and the sides of the wound flap up and down with rapid, feverish breaths. How horribly the body is made! If you poke it through there's a kind of bloody softness, and then there's something separate—the liver? the heart? a lung? What is that naked bloody thing that lies open in the living body of the wolf? Why doesn't he howl? Why doesn't he yelp or howl?

The horses whinnied, gave a tug. The wolf rocked at the strong jolt. Is that how they'll shake him and toss him around for the hundred versts to the tsar's park? I started howling wildly, a frenzied, animal howl.

"Vera, Vera!"

Someone was running toward me. Everyone was running toward me. But I ran from them straight toward the forest. I leapt across a broad ditch filled with water, forced my way through bushes, and crashed into the net. I fell. What thudded down onto me? Footsteps nearby. I wanted to jump up and run farther away from them, from people. But my hands were bound, my feet all tangled. The net, the net had fallen onto me from above. The net had me entangled.

Then I was seized with rabid horror, and started to lash out, bellowing and whooping, kicking, thrashing my arms, biting. At first there was laughter around me, then it died down. They were frightened. Someone said:

"She's gone mad!"

And Miss Florry's voice:

"That's a wild animal, not a girl. At least once a month she turns into an animal."

These words startled me, and suddenly I was quiet. Maybe it's the truth, and I'm a little bit animal. Not only a girl, but a little bit—animal. Once a month—I'm a beast. It made me depressed and suddenly I was tired. They untangled me. They were already cracking jokes. Already leading me submissive and silent toward the wagon, and cracking jokes.

I asked to sit by Fedor on the running board by the coach box. With him I felt more at ease. For a long while we were quiet. I forgot to ask my friend for the whip. I was thinking. Then:

"Fedor, it's good that they round up all the wolves. It's a good tsar who ordered them to do it."

"Sure it is!"

"Well yes, sure it is. Of course. Those wolves, they're really mean. They tear up the peasants' sheep, and even Golubchik, too . . ."

I'm beginning to cry.

"Fedor I *don't* like wolves. You shouldn't feel sorry for them."

"Why should you feel sorry for wolves, Verochka? Hey, you monkey around, Malchik! You want some whip?"

"Fedor, will you give me the whip?" I ask timidly.

He gives it to me. I wave at Malchik with the whip, aiming so that Krasavchik won't notice.

"Fedor, so now it'll be nice in the forest, without wolves? Now nobody will eat anybody else up?"

"Eat? So what are they suppose to feed on, the animals? Everybody feeds on somebody else, that's just how it is."

Fedor laughs sideways at me. He's joking. I'm getting bored. But Fedor's just getting warmed up; he's thinking it through out loud.

"And no matter how quiet looking a little animal is, not worth looking at, still it'll feed on somebody. That's because if you don't eat you'll die from hunger. Even a little piece of grass, it smothers the other one. That's how it is. Same way with man. Only animals eat just any old thing, but God told man what meat's clean, what's unclean . . ."

I'm curious.

"What do you mean, God did?"

"Very simple. Because God put man above all the animals and told him all he needed to know about the animals."

I'm bored again, since I've lost all hope of understanding anything. Fedor can only talk sensibly about horses.

"Fedor, hey Fedor!" I give Krasavchik a whip; he's hitting with his back leg and coming through the trace.

Fedor's angry. He has to get down. The horses are pulling. Krasavchik neighs.

The whole aristocracy, including Emma Yakovlevna, climbs out of the wagon with exclamations of fright.

Only Miss Florry remains seated, unperturbed.

And on the running board by the empty coach box, I hold the reins, pulling at them with all my strength. My hands are very strong.

"That leg . . . oomph . . . !" Fedor pleads with Krasavchik in his high-pitched tenor.

"That leg . . . oomph . . . that leg . . ." From the running board my bass comes in to help.

We're off again. Feeling guilty, I no longer dare ask for the whip.

"Fedor, hey Fedor, you know what? It makes me feel bad that everybody has to eat everybody else. It's boring, Fedor."

"Well, never mind. Why let something like that make you bored? That's just how it is. The animal, now he's without sin. We're the only ones who are sinful."

I didn't understand.

"Well, but what does it matter that we're sinful?"

"Well, then, we need to repent."

"Well, so?"

"Well, now that only God knows. Even death isn't fearful for an animal, see, because, like I explained to you, an animal has no sin. Man's the only one has to worry about death."

Up to then I had never had such an important talk, and Fedor's unexpected words so absorbed and surprised me that all my thoughts turned to something else. I was silent now, because I could find no words for those strange, important new thoughts. There was just one question that lingered, although it was shameful to ask it of the stern Fedor.

"Well, but what does it matter that we're sinful? What does it matter that we're sinful?"

I kept thinking that he would answer it, "Well that's just it. We're sinful, and that's it."

The alley to the house ran uphill, and the closer we got the steeper it went. But the horses sensed rest near at hand, they knew the stables were near, with their spacious stalls and paddocks. They sped upward with the heavy wagon. "How peeved they'll be when they let us out, at the big house, the estate people, and then still have to drop the village aristocracy off at their houses."

Old Elenushka, the maid, and the nurse had already rolled Mama's wheelchair out onto her sunny balcony. She herself sat there, leaning back wearily on the high sloping back, thin lids lowered on her dark blue eyes with their large whites. I crept up and started to kiss her thin eyelids. She didn't budge. Her heart must have told her it was me.

"Mushka, did your heart tell you it was me?"

Then I kissed her hands, on the thin palms now, and thought, "How prettily I said that to Mama." She smiled.

"How was it on the hunt?"

I turned a bit gloomy.

"Oh nothing much. They caught a lot of wolves. Only it's not nice at all. They poked a hole in one wolf's side with a rake. He was breathing through the wound . . ."

But I break off: Mama is very sick. She might have the same kind of stroke again, like the one that took her legs away . . .

"Poor creatures!" she says, immersed in thought; her face is so pale, so pale.

"But it's fine in the forest, Verochka, in the morning, so early! Does the morning frost bite? How I did love it."

"Oh Mama, what pine mushrooms I found! I'll get them right now."

I run off for the mushrooms. They're tied up in a scarf. Mama unties the scarf with clumsy fingers, admires them, smells their fresh rooty scent like a bouquet.

"Now I was never good at gathering mushrooms. I've got short-sighted eyes."

"Is that why yours are such dark blue? Mama, I can see myself in your pupil. In both your pupils, Mama!"

"Isn't Mariia Nikolaevna expecting you for a lesson?"

That was the village teacher with the braid; she gave me lessons in summer and fall.

"Not yet! She comes after dinner . . ."

"Of course. My memory's getting worse, too, Verochka. I get so mixed up. Soon I may get completely stupid . . . But you'll remember your other Mama, won't you Verochka?"

The corners of her lips quiver. How I fear it when the corners of her lips quiver. I'm already set to cry. I'm about to, but then remember that it's bad to upset Mama. I steel myself and whisper, not trusting my voice:

"Yes Mamochka, I will. I know who you are. Mamochka, why does Fedor say that animals aren't afraid to die?"

"How does he know?"

"He says they're without sin."

"Oh! that's true."

"But what about people?"

"People also don't have to be afraid . . . If they've understood."

"Understood what?"

"If they've suffered a great deal and have understood that one needn't have passionate attachments."

"What does that mean?"

"Oh, Vera, I want to talk with you like a big girl! You try to remember this, perhaps my life, useless as it is, will after all be of use to you. But I must hurry to get it said, because my illness is the sort that little by little will spoil not just my legs, but my mind . . . Do you know what it means when there are two people living inside one person?"

"Two . . . in one? . . . Mamochka, it's always like that . . ."

"There you are, you feel it, too! Well, in me it's always been that way. One person was always passionately attached, was greedy and ungenerous, wanted things for herself and didn't know how to give things away. Attached to, well . . . my big flower garden, or to coffee with thick fresh cream, or to the little down pillow under my head, or to my Golubchik or to Volodenka, your dead brother, and then to his grave, to this old house where your father was born and lived, and where I was . . . happy . . . before he left us . . . and then to my old Elenushka, the way she always gets my underthings ready . . . clean and comfortable . . . and to our ravine, to the Abramov spring . . . or even to the lime tree in front of the annex . . . ! It's all one and the same. It's all just passionate attachment; that first person gets attached. But then there's a second person, who is very free and who only knows how to love but has no passionate attachments. And that person in me spoke up very rarely. I rarely knew how to listen to her, when I was healthy. But when I took to my bed forever, then I heard her. And the garden became dear to me, and Elena, and Volodya's grave with the little flowers, or even just with wild grass, is dear, and your papa far away is precious and blessed, and our old house, and the children, you, who are alive—all of that has become dear to me in itself, and not just for me: there's come to be more freedom in my love, rather than attachment. And nothing can contain me anymore."

Mama laughed quietly, with a cooing sound.

"Does that seem silly to you? No? Not yet. It's still pure truth. But now I'll start saying silly things. Still you must believe it, even if it's the last thing, still believe it. Here I can't even go to the balcony railing by myself. If I could get out of the wheelchair, right away I'd stumble and fall, but even so, without my legs, I can walk out freely into our ravine or to the hay meadow, and not just that, I can go all over Russia, over the whole earth, through mountains and villages and cities, into the monasteries and wild forests . . . I'll go like a homeless beggar, without possessions, not tied down, and I'll help people with a thoughtful word, with my free, strong hands; and I fear nothing, not cold, not hunger, not death. Every tree is my father, every old woman I meet is my mother, every innocent beast, who lives by the earth, is my brother, and the grass is my sister . . . And sons and daughters—all God's children on the earth, and you, my loved ones, are also in my heart. For there's an endless amount of room in the human heart, and there's more of love's flame than is needed to set earth on fire, but that fire of love does no harm, like the burning bush, the fire did no harm, but burned, and has not burned out . . . That is the second person, Verochka: he loves, but without attachment, he is free. And my soul depends on my love, not on my legs. And that's why I say that even though I can't reach the railing, I've traveled the whole earth, I am traveling it. Do you know, Verochka, I've become a completely different person since I got sick. Alone here I've thought over a great deal, Verochka, and now I've told you everything at once. It doesn't matter that the sickness advances and my soul will grow dark again. Once you have had a glimpse, you will come into your new world . . . Now why are you crying?"

"I feel sorry . . . for the wolf . . ."

"You silly!"

Mother kisses me.

"Is it really all that dreadful to suffer? It's more dreadful to watch and feel pity."

"I feel sorry . . . that you're going to die."

"So that's it, that's what you were hiding, my clever Verochka!"

And Mama laughs.

"Is it really so important that we die? Or live? We only live in order to understand. If you've understood something, then that's enough. The spark has caught and rushed on . . . Where does it come from? Where is it going? How joyful not to know and to have faith. To love God so much . . ."

Suddenly Mama started to cry. For a long time she was silent. Something in her face grew stiff. And she started to cry and called out in an old and tinkly voice quite unlike her own:

"Elena! Elena!"

The nurse came up, but Mama waved at her angrily . . . Her lips were tired, they had grown heavy and shook. The skin around her eyes wrinkled up, she grew old, and tears stole down the wrinkles and spread along them . . . It was an attack of the darkness . . .

Or do I remember that from later years and connect it to this conversation? For at that time I didn't grasp those words.

But now I am grown, and my life, christened with pain, guilt, the ecstasy of happiness and bitter separations, has brought up those opaque, distant words from memory . . . There are certain pictures for children—I loved them as a child—magical pictures: the paper is opaque, you can't make anything out beneath that glimmering opacity; you put it in water and place it in your notebook, rub on top with your hand and take it off—out of the enchanting hiddenness emerge flowers, tender and brilliant.

»»» ««««

Deaf Dasha

There were two Dashas that lived with us: Deaf Dasha and plain old Dasha. Deaf Dasha was the daughter of the luckless widow woman who kept livestock on our estate. Her husband, a shepherd, had been butted to death by one of the young estate bulls. My mother paid for eight-year-old Dasha, almost the same age as me, to be taken in at the county school; the foolish bull had a flat board fastened to his filed-down horns and was let out with the herd again.

On our evening walks my governess kept well away from the earthen road where the large estate herd, with its pedigreed bulls, returned from pasture at sunset. But I felt drawn to that broad road, trodden on both sides; we argued each evening about what we wanted. I would say:

"There are waves on the road there; it's like Dolgovo!"

I loved the sea at Dolgovo and the wet, white, fine sand in which waves had pressed deep, sinuous furrows.

The furrows on my beloved road were deeper, and the waves of dusty manured earth between them flatter and broader, but still my heart stopped, overcome with unleashed memory of the sea. My thoughts transported me to the delights of those three unfettered weeks in July. We passed them without order or law in my Dolgovo. I would run there for hours, barefoot on wet stones; there we slept in haylofts.

"That is because your cows all move at an even, slow pace—stepping on the hoofprints of those in front: therefore furrows have formed in the dust and manure, reminding you of the sea with their wavy lines."

And then the governess recalled what had happened and added with subdued indignation:

"And it is remarkable how the best of people are ruined by wealth! For it's a crime to let such an accursed bull run free."

And I feared the evil bull that had butted Dasha's father to death, and at the same time something drew me to him, some burning curiosity, some eager recklessness.

But the next summer he suddenly threw the herdsboy on his board with such force, and so high, that when the boy landed on the rocky pasture land he broke his leg and three ribs.

The broken leg didn't surprise me, but the three broken ribs were so surprising they frightened me, and for a long time I couldn't sleep at night and lay crying about the herdsboy.

They locked up the bull in the barn, and there he roared, muffled exhausted groans. It was terrible and depressing and pitiful.

My three boy cousins arrived, the ones with whom I played reckless games of horses: the coachman would beat the horses pitilessly with a belt strap on the calves; meanwhile, the horses kicked the coachman, unstintingly, on the shins with their socks and heels. We all went into the livestock yard to see the bull in the barn. We found the barn by his dull, angry bellow.

"He growls like a lion," said my oldest cousin.

One after the other the cousins clambered up onto the ledge of the barn window.

"It's got the most terrible bull face," the middle cousin whispered down to us, and quickly jumped back down. "He has bloody eyes and a short neck; he's just waiting to strike. And there's no board at all on his horns! Why did you lie, Verochka?"

Then, when the youngest cousin jumped onto the window ledge, he called down to us:

"So which of us is ready to jump down there with him?"

I was just about to punch the middle cousin, for his insulting disbelief of my stories about the board on the bull's horns, but my youngest and favorite cousin's suggestion distracted me from the offender. I was already up there beside him—and, hooting at the top of my lungs, I plunged through the narrow window and came down at the legs of the startled bull. In an instant I had jumped up off my knees, in the next—I darted mouselike under the gate where it didn't hang flush with the ground.

I was already back with my cousins in the yard. They looked at me with embarrassed delight, while beside them stood the estate livestock keeper, hands clasped high, skirt tucked above her knees over dirty bare feet. She yelled at me in a thin wailing voice, and beside her, out of a pail thrown on its side, flowed a stream of milk onto greasy, gleaming brown dung. And there stood a girl, with a prominent, stubborn forehead and prominent, listening, colorless eyes. She looked at me with those wild, huge eyes, attentive and listening. I understood then how one listens with one's eyes, and guessed by them that it was Deaf Dasha, the daughter of our livestock woman, the widow of the dead shepherd. And something in the face and in the capricious look caught me off guard.

It was an unhappy summer, that summer when I first saw Deaf Dasha.

In the spring of that year I knew sorrow for the first time. My Ruslan died, the gray donkey with the smooth soft muzzle; I loved to kiss him there between the two swelling nostrils edged with a rosy border.

My Ruslan, who had been given to me two years before his death, along with his dark-headed wife, Liudmila!*

They both had black crosses—a band along the back, crossed at the shoulders—and I remembered how a drunken peasant had scolded me for harnessing Christ's donkey to a cart.

"But the peasants are simple folk and don't understand" was what plain old Dasha—"educated," disdainful, citified—explained to me then.

I rode out lovingly on my gray friend with the prominent, obstinate, listening eyes and the long, sticking-out ears. And his girlfriend, Liudmila, ran behind, on her ungainly legs that didn't bend at the hooves.

Liudmila was ill and couldn't walk in harness. Ruslan was healthy but didn't want to walk in harness, and for long hours we haggled, quarreled, fought, and acted stubborn. And more than once I crawled out confounded and angry from under the cart, where it had toppled into a ditch with its four wheels up.

Ruslan cried in a funny way, straining and wailing, with a groan and a wheeze, and then it seemed to me that living was painful and difficult for him, that he was asking for something, howling about something, hopeless and wild. Then I would start to feel irked and sorry, and I almost hated him because I didn't like to feel sorry. It was too painful.

Ruslan loved Liudmila. Liudmila loved Ruslan. They stood in the meadow with their necks intertwined, nibbling each other in the withers and growling in a quiet, contented fashion, quite unlike donkeys. Ruslan and Liudmila were inseparable.

In the autumn before that ill-fated spring, I left for town with a

* Ruslan and Liudmila are named after Pushkin's fanciful poem (1820).—Trans.

heavy feeling of parting, just as before, just as always when leaving the country, but without any premonition of misfortune.

It was still winter when I found out that Liudmila had gotten strangled on a rope tied carelessly by the coachmen in a grove among the trees.

I cried bitterly at the ailing donkey's death, at her true friend's grief.

In the spring my brothers and sister and I drove up to the country house with our usual wild "hurrah," I jumped from the big carriage while it was still moving and tore off straight to the stables to my donkeys . . . to my donkey.

His paddock in the corner of the big stables, so intensely fragrant with steamy horse manure, was empty. And Fedor the coachman, aging and handsome, recounted to me in a flustered, stumbling voice how Ruslan had grown quite sad, how he'd gotten quite lean, how he'd gone inexplicably deaf just before spring, then lost the use of his legs and died.

I opened my mouth and started to wail. It was a bad habit, of an unforgotten childhood. I wailed without stopping the whole long road through the park, from the stables to the house. With that long, animal wailing I honored my dead friend's memory.

It was sad, that solitary summer, when I first came to know Deaf Dasha.

One more year must have passed before the winter I'm remembering now, because Dasha had already turned eleven. She was unusually tall for her years, and thin.

We lived in town, and both Dashas were with us that time: Deaf Dasha and plain old Dasha.

I didn't like plain old Dasha because she had strapping good health, was well nourished, clean, laughed loudly, tended to scoff, was sly, and liked fancy dress. For some unknown reason my heart didn't fancy all that.

And I didn't like Deaf Dasha because she had a stubborn prominent forehead, frightened eyes that were too bright, prominent and unpleasantly listening on her gray, pinched face with the two lengthwise wrinkles above the nose, hair the color of a bast mop, ears that were damp, flat, and wavy. Most important, they stuck out, and it was from them I discovered that ears go deaf from scrofula. I found it disgusting, but in some tormented, obsessed fashion it drew my attention.

And there were sudden vivid moments when I loved this Deaf Dasha; because in those vivid moments she suddenly reminded me of my donkey Ruslan, dead that spring of sorrow for his wife—the sick donkey Liudmila.

So when Dasha suddenly reminded me of the dead donkey, fixing her eyes and stubborn forehead unexpectedly on me, I remembered all the sorrow and all the questions I had lived through, and once again I wanted to wail, no matter we were in town, and I was frightened by my country desire, frightened by the unbearable pain that gripped my heart, and suddenly I hated Dasha and yelled at her.

"Go away, go away!"

And I ran away myself.

Nor did I like the city—there was no earth there. Only far, far away, on a street that wasn't yet built up, you could stand at a chink in the fence, and ignoring the goading and reproofs of the governess, look at the poor gray earth, littered with bricks and garbage, there, beyond the fence, over there.

And nor did I like our city life. Family life exhausted my father. When he wasn't lying for days on end in his great wide bed, he would go somewhere far away, and my mother raised my older brothers and sister alone. In fact I no longer knew who was raising whom: they were considerably older than I and did what they wanted with themselves and with her, and with our life . . . I was alone.

And nor did I like our city apartment. It was very big and long on three sides, in the shape of a capital U. Only all three sides were even, the middle was maybe even a bit longer. All the "master's" rooms were in the middle part: the receiving rooms and my mother's and sister's bedroom faced the street, the other bedrooms and my two older brothers' studies faced the courtyard. In the right arm of the U were the kitchen and rooms for the cook, the men servants, and the dishwasher. In the left arm were the laundry room, a room for the laundress and plain old Dasha, and a dark corridor thickly populated with cockroaches; at the end of it, by the back entrance, behind a curtain, was Deaf Dasha's bed, and at the beginning was the door into my schoolroom and my governess's room, attached to it.

Two steps led down from the dusky storeroom into our dark corridor. I never walked through except on tiptoe, afraid of crushing cockroaches.

It was stupid to be afraid of cockroaches, but I couldn't help it, and the tall, red-haired exterminator, with his little bags in one hand and tin container in the other, seemed to me the most mysterious and unafraid of creatures; he would appear in our dreary corridor once a month, and each of his arrivals brought me the ruthless, futile hope that I would be spared my enemies.

The cockroaches didn't disappear . . . once they'd had their sweet, drugged sleep, the cockroaches awoke more energetic than usual, and, as before, I sprinted in horror the few steps separating the schoolroom door from the stairs to the brighter storeroom, where I played "gymnastics school" between solitary classes with my ten little balls of all ages.

We were being charitable to Deaf Dasha. I heard that from plain old Dasha and from Mama. As consolation for her father's having been butted to death by our estate bull, we were not only paying tuition and board for three winters' schooling for Deaf Dasha; now that the schooling was over, we'd taken her into the big house as a housemaid helper for plain old Dasha; we were clothing her and feeding her and giving her shoes. We were treating her scrofula with fish oil.

Dasha smelled unbearably badly of fish oil and sour sweat.

Once Mama said that Dasha sweated from weakness and soon showed her to our regular household doctor, to Fedor Ivanovich himself. After that they started giving her iron pills.

The strapping, attractive, plain old Dasha cleaned bedrooms in the "family" part of the house. Deaf Dasha had our corridor and the rooms that led off it. She cleaned our clothing and boots—she was our maid. Everything was in order, everything was as it should be, and yet from time to time an uneasy mix of pity, love, and hate troubled me when I looked at the gray, sickly, quietly listening face of our servant girl Dasha.

"That Dasha is an old lady and not a little girl!" our governess said once, and it stuck with me.

And another time:

"That Dasha is stubborn as a donkey!"

And once Sister said:

"That Dasha has no sense of gratitude whatsoever!"

And my older brother:

"That Dasha smells like my hunting boots when they're smeared with train oil!"—and then laughed good-naturedly at his own joke.

While Mother smiled apologetically and explained in her defense, "That's just from the fish oil."

"And from sweat," my severe younger brother added angrily.

"Sweat is from weakness, isn't it, Mama?" I asked, happy that I knew Mama's answer in advance.

I loved to ask questions when I knew what people would answer.

I loved to tease and make believe. I loved to steal into "family" rooms against the rules and hide there from the schoolroom, from the governess, until they would find me and put me back where I belonged. I loved to pilfer the sweets that lay in tantalizing abundance in the "family" rooms, and I pulled it off with great agility, so that I only got caught once.

That had happened three years ago, when I was nine years old. But I remember it well—and despite the clarity of my recollection, that sin was far from my last sin.

A box stood on Mother's table. In the box were chocolate candies with nut fillings inside. I came in to kiss Mama. The governess had just let me go after dictation.

(Oh, how honest she was, how tall, thin, clean and stern, my patient, serious governess, and I loved her and she loved me, but nonetheless, how often I declared that love without response from her, clinging, hopeless and mournful, to her brutal, evenly breathing chest.)

I came in. Mama wasn't there. Mama was somewhere else, somewhere with my sister: my sister's seamstress was there in the boudoir . . .

So . . . I should run to the parlor where the piano stood and practice my music lesson. I saw the chocolate . . . I stopped. If you break off the corner of a candy, the nut filling shows yellow under the dark chocolate crust. Yesterday evening, once she'd said prayers with me (I slept in Mama's room although I went to bed and got up earlier than she did), Mama gave me one like that, and the nut filling crunched against my teeth.

I thrust my hand toward the box and ran to the door with a candy already clasped in my palm, then down the corridor toward the parlor.

I played.

The candy, long since eaten, wasn't sweet.

I pressed four flat and stubborn fingers on the keyboard, and lifting the fourth one—the one that had no name, the lazy one, that seemed grafted onto the third—hit it dully against the key.

And I was angry . . . and felt miserable in a dull, exhausted sort of way, as always during the piano hour . . . I scowled and knit my brows so that I didn't notice when Mother came in and my sister with her.

"Liza, tell me: did you touch the chocolate candies on my table?"

Mother asked my sister knowing what the answer was, and I knew the answer, and of course Liza did—and this time it was horribly unpleasant that we all three knew. Why bother asking?

All the misery and irritation that seized me from that moment was contained in the pointlessness of that question.

"No, Mama!" and Liza looked down, blushing from a strange sense of duplicity.

"Vera, did you eat the candy?"

"No, Mama! . . ." I remember the dull venom of my stubborn voice.

Then I remember my father's vacantly large room, uninhabited once again, suffused with the sharp smell of tobacco. Once I'd confessed, I knelt beside Mother before the high empty bed that was covered in white, and she prayed:

"Dear Lord, teach her not to steal, teach her not to lie. Teach her to preserve her soul for You and for Your Truth."

And so forth and so on, at length. Then she chastised me and cried a long time . . . I don't remember her words, just that great sin begins with small ones, and that no matter how small the theft, it's still a great sin.

I was crying, too. And then we said the Lord's Prayer.

". . . Lead us not into temptation, but deliver us from evil."

And then Mama left, her eyes all red from crying, advising me to think, and closed the door.

And I did think for a long time, diligently chasing rebellious thoughts away; then I stopped thinking—I was tired of it, crawled up on the high bed and did somersaults for a long time, till I tumbled off onto the floor. I didn't climb up again but went off to search the room for new diversions. In my grandfather's large, heavy desk, with its numerous cunning drawers and hinged doors, I found one drawer not shoved in. I pulled it out, squeezing my thin fingers painfully through the crack: there was black powder sprinkled around my father's snuff box. It was snuff! When Father lies depressed, sometimes for days on end, he sniffs tobacco, and his eyes are so meek, so mournful! Then when I say good morning, pressing up against his long, quite silken, ticklish, silvery beard—then it smells just that way . . . just like the snuff box. Dark blue enamel on gold, with a portrait of a man with a scythe, nicked a bit on the gleaming smooth surface . . . And little stars . . . gold against the dark blue, like the sky, only at night. When Father took snuff, his sneezes were so loud and funny.

I reached for the snuff box, threw open the heavy gold lid, then sniffed up a black, pungent pinch from clenched fingers, and sneezed.

I'm standing and sneezing. Standing and sneezing.

And as I sneeze I jump up on tiptoe. I'm so happy.

I like it: you feel kind of pleasant all over your body, it's fun and easy to inhale, and I sniff up some more, sneeze again, jump up and down and laugh.

The room is blurry from my tears, I can't see anything, and sneeze . . .

Something lands on my shoulder . . . a hand on my shoulder, and suddenly my mother's face is close above me: "Is *this* how you think? Is *this* how you're repenting?"

And Mama is sorrowful, sorrowful and quiet, unyieldingly quiet . . .

They brought a screen into the schoolroom. Behind the screen they put my bed and my washstand. I didn't sleep in Mama's room anymore.

Soon I would turn eleven. Deaf Dasha was twelve years old, "already going on thirteen," as plain old Dasha put it, cursing her as a "big lazybones."

We were both girls, both of our mothers were far away: hers was in the livestock yard in the country, mine was in the receiving rooms, in the "family quarters" . . . Both regarding each other mistrustfully, with secret thoughts.

"You're like dear old Ruslan the donkey, who went deaf and died," I think, feeling sorry, not wanting to.

I don't want to feel sorry because it's painful to feel sorry . . . And I hate it.

Why does she have those white eyes—that's not like Ruslan— they're just sticking out and shortsighted like his, and they look at you the way he did—stubborn and listening? And why are there disagreeable wrinkles on her sticking-out forehead? Dasha's an old lady! And what disgusting ears! Plain old Dasha said "her ears drip," Deaf Dasha's do. How can they drip? And then she said it's from scrofula, she'll go completely deaf, "then what will you do with this prize?" She's nasty; that is, Deaf Dasha is nasty, not plain old Dasha, plain old Dasha is plain old mean.

Sunday evening when I was going to sleep, all alone, before my governess had returned from friends, I told her she was stupid, my governess. Dasha told the governess herself what I'd said, and after a family council I was locked for two days in the schoolroom, not allowed to come out, even to the dining room.

After that, when I met that jolly, strapping smart aleck I ran at her, grabbed on to her sides with my hands, and kicked her painfully with my hard heels: I'd been taken on a walk for the first time after my lockup, and had on my thick, dress-up walking shoes, built to last. It hurt her, the smart aleck.

My governess could barely tear me away. Righteous anger turned me into an animal.

Then I cried bitterly, said my prayers: my anger was righteous, but why, then, was I ashamed and hurting—no doubt hurting more than she had?

Soon after that it was my birthday.

There were lots of presents.

A big ball for the "gymnastics school," three times bigger than my head, or even Dasha's head. Really, Deaf Dasha's head was so ugly, so stupidly big and heavy on her completely thin, feeble shoulders. Why was she always silent, suspiciously and stubbornly listening with her white eyes?

Besides that, I was given a workbench for sawing wood, an English whip for riding in summer. Summer! And it's already spring! And this year they'll let me go riding on Cossack, Father's old horse.

They gave me a lot, lot more that birthday, I don't remember it all. And the governess gave me a whole set of portraits of Russian writers. That was boring. I didn't like to read. To live, to live, to live, like a wandering princess!

To live in the summertime with all my animals in the country. I had lots of them. But in the winter I was depressed and waited for spring, for the first green sound of a shepherd's pipe at dawn: even the morning light seemed green to me then, when I awoke to the first clatter of the city flock with their poor soft hooves on the stony road. Spring, and then it will be summer, and green joy . . .

They gave me a box of candies, too, real ones, the most fancy candies with chocolate and crystallized pineapple, a big box. It stood on my schoolroom table in the evening when I did homework till bedtime, and I helped myself from the box whenever I wanted.

When I finished my homework, the governess and I went to drink evening tea in the dining room. We sat silent together in the large, empty dining room. The grown-ups in the family came later. Then I went to the drawing room to kiss them good night, and my governess waited in the door to take me to the schoolroom. I dashed through dreadful cockroach land and darted in the door of the quiet, quiet schoolroom.

Deaf Dasha had already aired the schoolroom and gotten it ready for sleep, had turned back the bed. She's not afraid of the small venting window. But her ears "drip." Maybe that's why they drip, because she's not afraid of the window?

Who turns back her bed? The cockroaches? I made jokes to myself and laughed at them myself, and shivered with fear up and down my spine.

"What's the matter with you, you're not going crazy or something? Only crazy people laugh to themselves!"

I didn't answer the governess, and kissed her after asking my usual evening question:

"Do you love me?" and held tight to the ticklish loops on her knitted shawl of shiny black wool.

"From the bottom of my heart . . . suffering . . ."

"Be quiet, be quiet."

My heart stood still and I pleaded . . . But she was unyielding.

"A little bit, then . . ."

"Be quiet, be quiet!"

I was crying.

"Then no!"

She's laughing, she's merciless.

I know it's not true, that she loves me, but it hurts me. I go to my bed in tears.

I look absentmindedly into my box, already there are few candies in it, only on the bottom. Absentmindedly I look through them, to avoid getting undressed. There are fewer there than when we went to tea. Where are the three cherry ones that you can see all the way through?

What unpleasant misgivings!

I didn't eat them, and she didn't either, the governess, that is. She wouldn't have eaten them, and, besides that, she was with me in the dining room . . .

"Elena Prokhorovna, did you take the cherry ones?" I asked my governess, and I knew the answer, and blushed from a strange sense of duplicity.

Elena Prokhorovna's even, sharp voice carried from her room:

"No, of course not, Vera. I only take them when you offer."

"But then . . . I don't understand . . . and the chocolate heart, too . . . they always have rum in them."

"Go to bed, you're already ten minutes late."

I couldn't sleep. For a long time I couldn't sleep, and then I slept fitfully.

Of course it was her, Deaf Dasha, little Dasha Deaf-one, it's her who stole the cherries and the heart. Her. But if it was the cherries and the heart today, then what about yesterday, what about the day before, and all the days when there were lots of them and I couldn't check?

Of course she's the one who makes a habit of stealing. Now it's candies . . . but great sins begin with small ones, and then, no matter how small the theft, it's still a great sin.

Deaf Dasha is already a great sinner. But what will happen from here on! And why not ask for one? Why doesn't she ever talk with me, and barely responds to all my questions? And she's angry.

She's deaf, that means she hears badly. Only plain old Dasha says she's pretending. That's true; of course she's pretending, if she's so sly she steals, so brazen she steals! If she was deaf she'd be afraid to steal, then someone would spy on her, would come up to the door without her hearing and come in right at the minute, at that very minute, and catch her at it.

Then what? They'd pack her off back to her mother in the cattle yard. Of course, she's already able to help her mother with the milking . . .

Milking . . . how fun that is! I know how to milk. Dasha's mother showed me how. Only not just any cow: the teats have to be soft. You have to put two fingers on firmly, and slip them easy down the teat without letting go so a stream pings into the milk pail, so it hits with a ring. Even for Dasha that would be more fun than working here.

To begin with, here she's the only girl, all the rest are grown up; then, no one likes her because you have to yell at her, because her ears drip, because she smells of the fish oil that plain old Dasha makes her drink—she started doing it for fun, for a laugh, but in the end it was just on principle.

And besides that: how boring, cleaning up other people's rooms! It's dirty and even . . . humiliating . . .

And, finally, this is town, and in the country there are horses, mushrooms . . . trees to climb . . . No, of course that's not for Dasha.

Milking—that's for Dasha. Only if you do it a lot, of course, you get tired. Because she's weak, she's sick a lot and lies about in the corner of the cockroach corridor alone. And how could she not be afraid?

They aren't afraid! Common people aren't afraid of cockroaches, common people don't want to ride horseback or hunt for mushrooms or climb trees . . . common people . . . Well, still and all her mother's there, and she wouldn't be alone. But common people . . . do they love their mamas?

Does Dasha love her mama, does she miss her? I think not.

All day long I was working out my plan. In the evening I hid in the classroom, in the wardrobe. I was a frequent visitor in this wardrobe of mine. I dreamed there, I wept there, I found safety there from reproaches and persecution.

Through the crack I could see the table and the open box of candies. And Dasha thought I was in the dining room. I had discussed everything with Elena Prokhorovna. She was the one who first said:

"If you're going to accuse her, you must be absolutely certain."

"What does that mean?"

"You haven't seen her?"

Then the idea came to me; I told her, and Elena Prokhorovna approved it but asked:

"And then what do you want to do?"

I didn't know. I was flustered.

"I . . . I'll jump out and scare her. For the rest of her life she'll—"

"No, no, no! She's a sick girl, she has bad nerves. That's dangerous!"

Bad nerves? Mama's the one with bad nerves, but is it possible for common Deaf Dasha to have bad nerves?

"Well, then I'll jump out afterward and chase her down, and—"

"And then what?"

"Well, I'll say prayers with her!"

"In the corridor?"

"Well, yes."

"But isn't that where your cockroaches are?"

I thought it over, and suddenly something inside me got all fired up, and I whispered:

"Yes, let there be cockroaches. Am I afraid of cockroaches when God is there? We'll both say prayers. We'll both kneel and pray, 'Lead us not into temptation'—"

"*Us?* But you're not the one who stole the candies?"

I was flustered, and the fire inside me went out.

"Well, what about it? . . . I'll simply teach her how to pray, when she sees a box like that some other time and wants—"

Elena Prokhorovna laughed evenly and sharply, and I took offense and left, stamping my foot unevenly on the way to show my anger, and to have an excuse, in case I was scolded, that I had gone to my room "just so," and wasn't at all cheeky . . .

From the crack I saw the donkey-brow at my table and heard Deaf Dasha's heart beating above my table . . . or has memory mixed in the pounding of my own heart in the wardrobe? . . . and I saw how the sticking-out blue-white eye listened, how the white, perpetually chapped lips were clenched. A dirty red hand reached out and then snatched back with its loot. Then one more time . . .

And Deaf Dasha ran out of the room in a funny way, skipping like a goat, like I'd never seen her.

Is it possible that housemaid helpers skip?

But I hurried after her. By the end of the corridor I'd caught up with her. I put a hand on her shoulder and started to talk. I remember that my voice broke off, I remember it wasn't my voice. I listened to it and thought about the words, so stupid, disloyal, and false.

"Each sin is a small one at first, and then it's big, Dasha . . ."

She's deaf. I was speaking too quietly . . . I started to yell.

"First you'll take a candy, and then my whip (no, Dasha doesn't ride horseback), well, there's the ball (no, Dasha doesn't play), well, anyway. Then it'll be money . . . then you'll land in prison!"

Enough. I yelled about prison quite terribly. But Dasha kept silent . . . She kept looking at me up close, without blinking, and breathed fish oil on me out of her chapped white lips. What more can I yell?

"I saw, Dasha, I saw it myself! I was in the wardrobe . . ."

Suddenly I blush. It's dark here and you can't see my face—but why should I blush?

"Dasha, let's say a prayer!"

And I fall to my knees and pull at her skirt, although I had always fastidiously avoided touching Deaf Dasha. But Dasha stands like a wooden idol and doesn't want to kneel.

Is it possible her mother hadn't taught her to pray? Common people probably don't teach their children to pray. No breeding—there you have it.

I prayed.

"Lead us not into temptation . . ."

And I begged Dasha to repeat my words.

"It will help you, it always might, poor Dasha, another time when you want to take what's not yours . . . I know myself. I . . ."

I hesitated. What had I said? What did I want to say? Could I say something like that to her, to this Dasha, was it any of her business?

What business? Precisely what tormented me so, tormented me so horribly: that I was a thief, that I was thief, that I myself was a thief!

Because at my sister's wedding I had hidden a whole silk bag of candies in the storeroom, in reserve.

And Dasha suddenly threw her bony red hands to her face and started to wail, just exactly as I had in the spring, when I'd found out in the stables about Ruslan dying. My heart stood still from Dasha's wailing, just stood in my chest.

"Oh God! Oh God! Oh God!"

And I let go of Dasha's hem, because she tore it out of my convulsively clenched fingers, and jumped up from my knees, and we ran off toward different ends of the cockroach corridor.

Shameful, shameful, shameful! Once again I sat in a wardrobe, but not in mine, now that I had let Elena Prokhorovna in on the secret of my wardrobe; I sat in the large wardrobe, stuffy with the silken party skirts hung there, in the storeroom. There, in the very corner, completely small, a small hunted animal, a small frightened animal, I didn't cry there but sat motionless; my eyes opened wide and I looked motionless at the dark wardrobe, into the dark pleat of silk that hung by my nose, pressed close against my nose.

Shameful, shameful, shameful! Shame pursued me as a hunter pursues an animal. It's good that it's quiet. It's good that it's dark. If only they wouldn't find me, if only they'd never find me.

Was it hours that dragged on, or minutes? Busy footsteps went past, returned, then moved away again . . . Then everything grew quiet. The little light in the keyhole went out. Then steps again, again the small light circle . . .

And light in the wardrobe, the old door creaked as it opened wide.

They looked for me, parted the silk skirts and found me . . .

I made my way to bed without explaining anything. I lay down without washing, foul-tempered, silent . . .

I'm not sleeping.

It's night already. I steal along the unlighted corridor. I clasp the box in my hand, the box with the rest of my candies.

There behind her curtain Dasha strikes at the light in fright. It's horrible for someone who's deaf to suddenly hear steps in the night.

Dasha sits there, white and thin on the dirty, gray bed, watching like a donkey with her sideways, obstinate glance, and her lips whisper something soundlessly. Dasha's rough blanket prickles me across the thin fabric of my shirt . . .

"Here, here! It's not mine!"

I throw the box toward her on the bed.

"I stole all of it. All my life I've stolen. I'm worse than you. Listen, Dasha, Dasha, I'm bad. Dasha, hey Dasha, can you forgive me?"

Dasha is silent. Or am I speaking softly?

I try to whisper to her clearly, distinctly, right into her ear. Oh, today I'm not afraid of her sick ears. I must, must say what has surged unexpectedly into my soul in an unrestrained river of love. It surged and flooded in me, muffled and indistinct still, but already the only thing, the truth, the truth for once and all.

"Dasha, you're a girl and I'm a girl!"

Dasha directs her obstinate gaze in silence, like a donkey.

Suddenly I hear a whisper:

"No, I'm not like that."

It means she'll talk. It means she hears me.

"Dasha, you have a mama and I have a mama. Dashenka, don't be angry anymore, believe me. Dashenka, I want to sleep with you in your bed and eat with you in the kitchen. I want to work with you."

I pulled at her, pressed her thin hands, her shoulders, her neck. She was softening, not like an idol. Now she smelled of fish, and sweat, and dirty linen.

"Dasha, I'll wash your linen. Dashenka, you know, I can't stand it anymore alone! Dasha, you have hands and eyes . . . you understand . . . I have the very same things. Look, look, I love you, little sister!"

And I kept talking and whispering a great deal, quickly, indistinctly, and I cried, and Dasha cried. Suddenly she dropped her stubborn forehead onto my shoulder, and I buried my wet face in her neck and it struck me quite clearly—

Exactly like my two donkeys.

And suddenly something inside me fired up, like yesterday when I talked about the prayer to Elena Prokhorovna over tea, and I said quite loudly—there was no one there, I wasn't afraid of them:

"Dasha, do you know how to say the Lord's Prayer?"

"I do."

"Who taught you?"

"Mama."

That means her mama had taught her to pray, and up to then I hadn't known anything about her mama.

"Dasha, pray 'Our Father, Who art in Heaven.'"

And Dasha prayed.

"Our Father, Who art in Heaven, hallowed be Thy Name. Thy Kingdom come . . ."

We knelt beside each other, with our bare knees on the cockroaches' floor, and Dasha prayed quickly, devoutly, lowering her forehead to the floor and crossing herself in broad, devout sweeps. But I didn't hear beyond the first words. I couldn't hear . . . My whole soul was filled with them, filled to overflowing . . .

"Hallowed be Thy name. Thy Kingdom come—"

"Dasha, Dasha, do you understand the prayer?"

"I understand it."

"Who taught you?"

"They taught us in school."

"Dasha, do you understand . . . Listen, Dasha, sweet Dasha, now understand what I'm going to tell you. Maybe no one will believe it but it's still true, what I'm going to say . . ." I was hurrying, gasping for breath—"that's what it will be, 'Thy Kingdom come,' when it's like what we wanted just now . . ."

And suddenly I jumped up. We sat on the bed, and I hurried to finish what I had been saying:

"Only we're not donkeys, Dasha. We won't be just the two of us; we'll love everyone: Prokofy and Ilya and the cook and Elena Prokhorovna and Fedor the coachman and my brothers and your mama . . . and plain old Dasha and the dishwasher. We'll all sleep and eat together, and we'll work together and . . . go riding . . . or we don't even have to. Even without that it will be incredibly fun, and the thing is it's so simple. And you know what? There'll be no point in stealing."

This thought set me laughing, and I laughed, happy.

Now Dasha looked at me, and I suddenly realized that what had seemed to me obstinate listening in her sticking-out eyes was fear. She watched and feared my words. She did not believe, she didn't yet believe. Then I kissed her eyes, still wet with tears, and the raw, bast-colored tendrils of her hair, and then looked again to see if she was afraid.

She kissed my hands, and I kissed her hands. How rough the skin on them was!

The dear, rough, blessed skin on Deaf Dasha's hands!

And now I am different. All of me, every last drop of me, is completely, completely different. I looked, as if for the first time. I looked at people and at the order of things for the first time and I saw, I saw simply, and understood simply, understood with every last drop of me that all of it—how people have set things up—isn't the real thing. And so it will not be that way, because I do not wish it.

»)»)» «(«(«

The Monster

*Dedicated to Konstantin Aleksandrovich Siunnerberg**

In the spring I caught a monster with a net in the bog.

It didn't come by itself. I brought it home in a small bucket, poured everything I'd caught into a jam jar, and put the jar on the small round table by the window in my room.

If you looked through the murky water toward the light, a whole bog world appeared there.

Some kind of whirlygig minnows, thin, almost transparent, with heads and whiskers, turned jaunty somersaults. Scratchy little sticks, like bits of narrow twig, went swinging forward, and suddenly a shaggy head emerged from one of their ends. A small snake cut the murk with an angular clearing motion, first gathering its tiny body in a rose-colored clump, then spreading it out in a slender thread.

Then there were lots of shadowy, incredible grubs, just awakening to life, which I barely remembered having caught; they shifted among the grasses at the bottom of my jar.

Jellylike frogs' eggs lay in dense clusters. Inside each murky green egg was a black seedlet-embryo.

* Konstantin Aleksandrovich Siunnerberg [Erberg] (1871–1942) was an art critic, a theoretician, and a contributor to the symbolist journal *The Golden Fleece;* his work elaborates a theory of intuitive creativity.

Soon the black seedlets started growing, and the egg jelly melted off somewhere. And suddenly I saw that each seedlet had grown a small tail.

Often I would come stand by my bog jar, watching the bog life, waiting: now I would see it, now it would begin. But nothing noticeable was wrong. I kept waiting for the monster to reappear.

I had seen him then for only one moment, that morning when a ray of sunlight suddenly illuminated the boggy murk, held in the net above the water but not yet lifted completely out; it had swum toward the top and then slipped once more into darkness.

Had I in fact dreamed him, but clearly, as things can only be when waking, not in sleep? Yellowish-brown, a small tough body of flat linked pieces, a strong rudder tail, and two claws coming out of the head, huge, strong, and round, with sharp linked tips. I observed it all in a sunny moment, despite the fact that the monster was no longer in size than one-quarter of my ten-year-old's pinky.

It lay in hiding three days or more, and I finally almost stopped believing I'd caught it. The net probably had a tear somewhere, or it had died in the jar. And I grew bored . . .

I longed to see the monster. And I did see him, of course.

It swam up once from the mass of frogs' eggs, quite unexpectedly, so that I cried out abruptly:

"There it is!"

My startled teacher asked severely:

"Who? . . . You frightened me."

I was silent. For some reason I never wanted to talk about the monster.

"What are you so happy about?"

Was I in fact happy? I hadn't known I was happy, and I looked once more at the disgusting flat body of links and claws, swimming slowly, with sinister confidence, steering true with its strong, sharp tail.

"I'm not happy," I finally answered decisively.

"Then why did you shout that way?"

"I found a monster."

Now my teacher laughed, with her mirthless, condescending laugh, and came toward me.

We stood in front of the jar and scrutinized it.

I found it revolting, but at the same time that fear and revulsion drew me to it.

"It's a disgusting grub!" my teacher said, after a long pause. "Throw it out. It will make all sorts of trouble here."

But I didn't throw it out, and *it* disappeared once more.

The frog jelly melted not by the day but by the hour, and, instead of the indistinct seedlets, fat black heads appeared, indisputably ugly and awkward, near the broad, transparent gray tails that I found so dapper.

They were tadpoles being born and swimming to freedom, lethargic, kind, soft all through and amusingly slow, despite the ardor of their broad, dapper, waving tails. They knocked awkward heads with a kind of trust and muddle-headedness; their muslin tails got entangled with the others'.

I loved them tenderly.

In innocence they grew, in innocence they fed—on what and how I had no idea.

I felt in them something akin to myself. I envied them, I disdained them, I loved them tenderly; yes, their silly fat heads, where, of course, there were backs and stomachs lurking; and their dapper, much too tender tails.

And they grew not by the day but by the hour.

The yellow-brown monster disappeared behind the fat, black host.

But it was strange: my tadpoles fattened and grew, but the herd grew inexplicably smaller.

And then I saw *it* a third time and at first didn't understand.

Already one-third the size of my pinky, it seemed enormous. The flat, rough body arched its linked back sharply upward, dropped its powerful tail like a stake, and as it paddled along with that rough tail, a different tail went down, its delicate muslin torn to shreds.

Then I saw both head and claws. The fat, silly, awkward head of a tadpole in the rough, powerful, piercing claws of the monster. And I understood.

I stared at the two bog brothers, held in such dreadful embrace.

"There's the trouble *it* will make," I recalled the teacher's words.

And suddenly my heart stilled completely, as though it had stopped and gone into hiding, heavy as a lead weight, frightened and greedy, strangely greedy.

I stood still that way for a long time, and for a long time the silent bog doings carried on, in the murk of the boggy jar.

The black body-head turned gray, its color grew closer and closer to that of the gentle gray tail, its form grew tapered, and the ragged little tail shook more weakly . . . stopped shaking altogether. The film of gray fell slowly to the bottom of the jar.

In the pond there is an island, quite small, all covered in resinous old poplars that hang right down to the water, quiet and dark.

I sit beneath a poplar on the narrow shore, by the water, dark and quiet. My small boat doesn't move; it's an old one, with worn-off paint that was once a festive color. The oar is tossed aside. I poled here with one oar, along the shallow pond's bottom, from the nearby shore.

So here I am, sitting in the shade above the water, and crying. There in the water move drowsy, lazing fish. For it's noon, and farther off, where the poplars' shadows don't hang along the water, the water is all overlaid with the thick viscous light of midday.

There are silver fish and thin ones—they're more lively—and then there are black ones with thick heads and bellies that sag downward. Those are quite like my tadpoles, only they're five times bigger and just as awkward, just sleepier, and their tails aren't like muslin.

So I cry and cry. Not bitterly or abundantly, just crying, also with a noonday laziness.

And inside me I feel quite sour.

"Vera! Vera! Not again!"

It's the angry, somewhat raspy voice of my older brother.

"Bring me the boat, quickly. Since when are you allowed on the island alone?"

"Mama let me yesterday."

"Well yesterday isn't today."

"She let me for today and tomorrow and forever."

But even as I'm shouting at the top of my voice, I'm in the boat and steering straight for my brother; I give a powerful shove and turn to the left from the stern like a wing, with my bow heading right. Quite a little minnow, I've grasped the long oar and turn with it. A shove to the right, a shove to the left.

To the right, to the left.

Uneven, impatient, shuddering passionately—just like my passionate, impatient, independent will—my boat flies up to the shore.

The bow has almost touched. My brother is already rasping out:

"Where are you going? Where? And they let you go out alone!"

"You've got the dogs!"

The two sleek setters, Piron and Boyar, and the long, wavy-haired gordon, Bertha, yelp by the water from excitement and nerves.

"What, you've only just noticed?"

"Are you going to let them swim?"

"Yes."

"Can I come?"

I look pleadingly into the boat, because I've long since shifted to the planks of the pier, and my brother is in the boat, in my place.

"You can't, somebody was looking for you at home. You still haven't learned some scales or other."

"Vasenka, Vasenka, please let me!"

"You can't, I tell you. I just remembered: it was Emilia Lvovna looking for you. She's in the drawing room, and she's very angry. I'd get a move on."

And then, quite gently, uncharacteristically, my brother adds:

"What's the matter, Vera? Were you crying? You're all puffy from tears. Were you punished?"

I flared up.

"Just the opposite."

"And what's the opposite of punishment? A reward? Think we'll live that long? Let's ask Emilia Lvovna at dinner, let's ask!"

Oh how I hate this Emilia Lvovna, the lazybones. She's only come to the country to give music lessons and she's ill-humored from boredom, thrusting sheets of music in my face!

But I don't want to tell my brother about *them* and about *it*. And I'm afraid to keep silent: won't he really start to believe it? I mean, won't he believe I'm being punished? Shame! Shame! And he's kind today, even though his teasing is unpleasant, like always, and his voice is tender, and he's become just like Mama himself.

"Vasenka, it's the tadpoles."

And once again I'm crying and telling him about them, and about *it*—the monster.

Vasya listens to me attentively, one foot planted on the bottom of the boat, the other thrust up on the high edge of the pier. Then for a fairly long time he's quiet.

And then quite resolutely he says:

"That's nature, Vera."

I don't know what to make of it.

"A normal person gets used to nature. It becomes like second nature."

I don't know what to make of it.

He notices my stupidity. He smiles at it condescendingly, but also a bit sadly.

"You see, don't you understand, all of that around us," he drew a big arc with his hand, "in the water, on the earth, and in the earth, understand? It all lives according to nature, understand, and that means it can't do any differently. And, as a result, that's how it has to be. Well, but people sometimes want to live in ways they can't. That means making things complicated, understand, and not even obeying God, understand, God!? So don't cry . . . Piron! Piroshka! . . . You'll get used to it . . . Boyarka! Bertha! Here! . . . There's no help for it . . . Into the water you cowards, you scoundrels! . . . So don't cry, silly girl!"

He rowed standing up, to see the dogs better; he quietly worked both oars, heading down along the pond toward the dam where the water was deep, and the two dogs' heads, their ears laid back, swam close behind the stern.

Only Bertha was still yelping and barking on the shore; she would run into the water up to her belly and jump back out, shaking off the diamondlike spray from her long, wavy hair. She looked up at me with her big brown eyes; they were guilty and frightened, greedily, restlessly beseeching. There was an exhausting, frightened longing in her bark and in the unpleasant twists and turns of her body, wet through and suddenly grotesquely thin.

My brother yelled wildly.

"Bertha! Come here, you bitch!"

With one leap Bertha is in the water. The long white back with a patch of yellow in the middle still trembles unevenly above the water. It's clear that her paws can still reach the bottom, they're stepping. But now the back has sunk under, only the patch just sticks out. Bertha swims evenly, effortlessly, and her luxurious tail lies on the water like a trusty rudder. Soon in the distance I can see only her white head, and with my too-seeing eyes I make out russet ears trembling with fright, glistening with sun on their long, wavy silk.

"Or you know what? Throw out your jar!" my brother yells, his overly loud voice traveling over the quiet water. "Faster, Bertha, faster! . . . Throw it in the wash pail . . . Hello, friends, after me! . . . What are you keeping slime in your room for?"

"Why don't you throw that disgusting grub out of the jar?" asked my teacher, quite unexpectedly interrupting the explication of Schiller's ballad "The Goblet."

I stared straight into her eyes, but didn't see them and didn't answer. She repeated the question.

"Because . . . that's how it has to be."

"What has to be?"

"That—so it will eat."

"And why is that?"

"That's how God made it."

"And who explained that to you?"

"Vasya himself."

And my eyes, still not heeding the tall, sinewy woman sitting opposite, grew hard and impudent.

Then I added with a laugh, drawling out my words:

"Because—that's nature."

"In no way is what you have in that disgusting stupid jar nature. It's plain old capriciousness."

She's very indignant. She's right and she's not right, because in the swamp there is more room for them to hide, but then there are more things to attack them.

So I say angrily:

"Well, so much the better."

Now I saw the eyes I'd been staring at so long, so impudently, without seeing. But the pale, unattractively flared-out eyes were unusually agitated, even frightened. My strict, righteous, extremely shortsighted teacher is frightened by sure signs of resurgent rebellion. Something pushed me to rebel. Words of some kind—incomprehensible even to me—squeezed upward and out of my mouth.

She kept on asking:

"What is better? Why is it better?"

"It'll end quicker."

"Dear Fathers! What will end?"

I didn't know what would "end," didn't know what and why it was "so much the better"; but I knew I would no longer read and explicate Schiller's "Goblet," with its repulsive sea monster. I stood up impertinently from my chair opposite her and, with an air of importance, walked out of the schoolroom unhurriedly.

I decided to head for the pond . . .

Of course after the pond I was punished: three days without playtime.

Now there were only thirteen tadpoles left, and nothing was left alive in the boggy murk except for them and the monster.

Perhaps not less than two weeks had passed since the day we read Schiller's ballad, and the tadpoles shown mercy were in essence no longer tadpoles. Four flared paws with tiny webbed fingers had grown out of each fat head. And the head itself proved not only a head, but had a soft little belly and a round-shouldered frog's back.

And I laughed aloud now at the frogs with tails. Why did frogs in the open, in the grass, not have tails, but in my jar they did?

My darlings, my darlings!

While the monster, who'd gobbled up everything that swarmed in my bog catch—like Pharaoh's seven skinny cows, who gobbled up seven fat ones and didn't get fat—stayed just as fat, rough and plated, with a strong, menacing tail and greedy claws. It just got a bit longer.

I came to love the monster.

To me it seemed clothed in armor. And in the soundless bog water murk, where soft-bodied, witless, quite defenseless tadpoles joggled and jostled, it alone ruled absolute over lives—precise, strong, swift.

And it devoured, triumphant.

And I disdained the tadpoles.

I would run, though, to the river and to the pond. I would crouch down and stare for a long time into the water. I was thinking of splashing it in there. In order to stop seeing it, and in order to save at least those thirteen tadpoles with tails.

Once more in the pond I saw black tadpoles, sleepy little fish. Maybe he'll start sucking them up? He'd grown to half the length of my little finger, the horrible thing.

And I returned to the jar empty-handed. There I saw the well-fed, lazy monster, nestled on the bottom among gray skins he'd sucked dry.

The monster was mysterious.

The teacher and I talked a great deal about him. We looked through three books where all sorts of things were described. We compared, we measured, but still weren't certain about his past, or his future.

"You know, I still think this grub of yours will turn into a water beetle!" the teacher announced decisively.

Then we both stood by the window and looked into the jar.

"Well, a water bug is black and round."

"So, what do you make of that?"

"It's not at all alike."

"Good Lord, how unreasonable you are! Do you think mosquitoes, that those silly stalks floating in your jar will turn into, look like their grubs? And butterflies?"

I'm not convinced.

"Water beetles are good."

"How do you know?"

"Down below in the barrels, you know, the ones under the gutters, lots of them swim around."

"Well, what of it? Have you gone swimming with them, like a little beetle maybe, or a fish?"

"Well, so what?"

"Why are you so sure they wouldn't eat you up?"

"Anyway, I don't believe that *it* is a water beetle."

"Well, I'm not certain either. Strange mysterious grub!"

The monster had to turn into something. But into what? What? What could things so evil, so brownish-yellow turn into, clawed and plated as they were, with tough tails that steer like a rudder toward the victim?

How terrible that the monster had to turn into something!

But maybe, after all, it would turn into a black water beetle, round, shiny and . . . maybe, probably even, of course, it would be good.

Where, then, would the evil go?

Could it disappear completely? Simply go nowhere, simply disappear? Like steam . . .

No, steam thickens from cold into clouds in the sky, and the rain comes down . . . Isn't that so?

Only one small frog was left. And at some point his tail had fallen off. He'd become such a fresh young thing! So, so dear! All green! With a strong back, feet spread wide and warty, with staring eyes.

He made it out of his homemade little bog by climbing up the glass; he breathed quickly, the way pocket watches whir, and his fat, soft little stomach fell in and rose at his short neck. He was so, so green and always fresh from a bath.

He watches wide-eyed with soft, crumpled lids. He doesn't climb down in the water.

Tame!

The monster?

So what am I to do with the monster?

Not in the river. Not in the pond. In the bog? There are baby frogs there, too.

I brought a rock for the jar, found a thick one and set it on end, so he could climb out on top. He has lungs now, he breathes with lungs now and not with gills. Both with lungs and gills: with whatever he needs. My teacher said so.

But he climbs down from the rock. He loves the water. And then . . .

To kill.

To kill the monster and save the soft, tame little frog, the last one.

But how to kill something so tough and plated? You can't crush it. It will crunch. It's impossible. Disgusting.

Simply catch it and shake it out in the sun. It's sunny on the balcony. There's a door right here from the room onto the balcony; strictly speaking onto the roof, which is railed off with a ballustrade and covered with iron sheeting. The iron heats up almost as much as my toy irons, which I use to press my doll's clothes. (I even tried to heat them that way in the sunshine.) That's the south. But even so, of course, for this one it's not enough . . .

Still, if you splash it out, it will bake to death there. It'll croak, the filthy thing.

Yes, Vasya was right. Better then to have poured it all together into a pail. Oh God! Why is it so hard?

Little green one sat on the stone till evening. Mouth like a rainbow, little warts everywhere. Looking. And then he lowers the soft folds over his eyes, and they become two stretched-out gray balloons.

I went about impatient, ill-tempered. My heart was in torment.

I loved and hated the monster.

No, I hated the green one.

I went to bed that way, without deciding. Anyway, toward evening the sun had left my balcony . . .

I'm lying down and trying to sleep, not sleeping. It's very unpleasant.

I should light a candle. To see what's in the jar. What if it doesn't sleep at night? Does it have eyes? I didn't notice behind the claws. And, anyway, it doesn't matter. Since at night your eyes can't see.

It will suck the frog to death. Oh, *it* will suck it to death before morning!

But the other one's on the rock . . . He'll climb down; oh, he'll climb down from the rock into his favorite murky water, boggy and homelike.

On purpose, I've been bringing water from a deep ditch, where slippery grass grows. Only I've tried hard not to scoop in a new creature together with the water . . .

My mind races and I've already lifted my foot toward the floor. Suddenly I remember angrily: "Nature! Nature!" "Man wants to live in ways he can't." "That means not even obeying God."

And then I'm lazy! And it's dark! And it's awfully unpleasant to see him at night.

But what if suddenly it changed? Suddenly right today? Right now has decided to change? And if it decided to change, maybe it's a sin to kill it. Maybe before it sucks the other one to death it will change, and then it will never suck anyone. But if I kill it? Kill it right at the moment when I shouldn't?

And then how to kill it? There's no sun at night. You have to crush it. It will crunch. It's hard.

I buried my head beneath the pillow, so everything would be muffled and soft.

So let it! . . . That's how it has to be.

I fell asleep.

In the morning, the goggle-eyed, web-footed little frog was no more.

It, it. It alone.

I don't feel sorry. I don't cry. Some sort of calm had descended.

I go down to the pantry for a spoon, in silence, biting my lip in businesslike fashion. I fish out the sleepy, well-fed monster with the spoon. And out onto the iron balcony.

The sun hasn't heated the iron sheets yet. It's still around the corner.

Shall I wait? Impossible!

I splash out the water, shake him out onto the floor. I watch.

He coils about, beating disgustingly with his hard tail against the iron, lifting his clawed head with its vile yellow eyes. I see, now I see everything. I lean over close. He'd be half the length of my little finger, but I imagine that I'm looking into his eyes, right into them, vile, yellow, greedy, merciless.

I brought the stone that had been in the jar, where the green one would sit. I pressed the stone on the vile head with its claws and eyes. I crush it. It crunches. But the plated body still shakes, curving all over, and the tail lifts upright.

It's unbearably disgusting.

I throw the stone. The head is all crushed.

Nothing. Nothing. Now everything will be finished. Still businesslike, I go to my room. I grasp the jar tight with two hands—and through the window.

The jar flies, splattering fetid, dead water, the dirty jar flies far beyond the window, toward the clean sand on the flower-bedded lawn. It's a heart that's grown spiteful, with a sharp feline claw.

Nothing. So everything in my jar "finished quickly." Let it.

But there, in the bog, it continues—as God ordained?

»»» «««

The Midge

Dedicated to Modest Liudvigovich Gofman*

I loved spring and hated it, not knowing what I loved, not knowing what I hated.

It was simply that mute tidings stole into my prison, one prison among many, my winter prison of stone, tidings that spring had come, and every drop of blood already knew it.

The hateful stone city, where even the mud wasn't real, not made of earth, where grass and trees were make-believe—suddenly the city itself became unreal and make-believe, as when you finish your lessons and you're still standing, listening to the governess's sermon, and you know that all the words being said are pointless and you don't hear them, and you know that you'll stand that way, still not listening, a bit longer, just a bit more, and you'll run out of the room, and the words will be forgotten, even the ones you didn't catch.

That spring, when I wailed for my sins, burrowed under Anna Amosovna's pillow—mute tidings of a thawing earth came unbearably

* Modest Liudvigovich Gofman, a Saint Petersburg editor who worked with numerous symbolist authors, was himself a writer and later a Pushkin scholar.

slowly. And the shepherd was late to drive his urban flock down our long street, toward bald pasture at the edge of town, where Anna Amosovna and I had already taken frequent jaunts after breakfast, in place of "gymnastics," always forgetting galoshes on purpose—to feel real earth with soles of feet all drenched on the dank spring road. And his raspy horn had not yet sounded, soft hooves had not yet beaten their earthen tread on the road of brick. And I didn't yet leap up in my bed, I didn't hear the country sounds with eyes wide open, my heart, startled with joyful anguish, was not yet bursting against the narrow cage.

The city hadn't yet let go; it still stood bound, its walls clenched wall to wall, hatefully real. And the days grew long, mornings were early and the twilights turned to white that changed to rose.

That spring the midge said spring to me, gave sudden freedom to a weary, waiting heart, one brief moment of freedom—one, no maybe ten, galloping freely with sudden joy, mad joy and rushing fear—ten thuds in my breast's left corner and . . . gone.

It was in the dining room at evening tea. The dining room wasn't light, the lamp above the large table was already lit, and the white tablecloth gave off a brilliant light. I noticed it on the brilliant, gleaming white canvas, at the very moment when transparent tiny wings released a small body, head the size of a pin, onto the tablecloth.

"A midge! A midge!"

And I all but expired in that briefest of moments, in that half-minute, as I gazed with sharp-sighted eyes at the dust-mote-midge, because suddenly the whole of spring burst out, in a heart that had been utterly empty. A spring so expansive, so fragrant!

And joy, the kind that shouts aloud, runs and shouts, runs and shouts. I'm the one running and shouting, but it seems as though everything does.

I run and shout. And in that instant my grove of spring existed. Through the green, breathing young shadow were golden shafts, generous, lush shafts of light. They touched the green grass and damp sand—and spread into liquid, abundant pools of gold.

A horse flies along: these are its slender, lithe legs, thrusting easily from damp, resonant earth, trampling it again in precise, playful rhythm. The legs are a horse's. The body is a horse's. But the head?—where dreams and images, origins and endings, swirl with the wind like butterflies torn free of cocoons? The head is mine.

But who am I? It doesn't matter. It doesn't matter. Spring is complete, blooming, resplendent.

How many times did I cry out at table, as the spring grove bloomed and the horse with my head went galloping in the early darkness of a city dining room?

"A midge! A midge!"

I think once. Maybe twice. And in that half-minute spring rolled past, leaving only the sound of its metallic wheels in besotted ears. Its marvelous large wagon rolled past, and the chill from its vanquished green branches still shivered on the lids of eyes deceived.

Anna Amosovna's sudden voice, and words stupidly direct.

"A midge? Where?"

The broad, dry palm of her flat hand slapped the living vernal dust-mote, and skipped flat along the table.

My mouth opened and the cry didn't come. It was only a whisper, reining in the wild wail of my last strength, what remained of my ecstasies:

"You've crushed her."

I jump up, run from the dining room, skirting the long empty table where the two of us had sat at the end, just us two. And then farther, along the interminable corridor, I carry my uninterrupted wail gingerly, like a bowl of soured milk. I won't spill it, I keep a tormenting balance in my fragile breast.

I'll take a breath and the wail will break out! I run without breathing.

Where to? The wardrobe? Everyone knows about the wardrobe. They'll head there first to find me. I'll have to find new shelter, where they won't think you can cry.

I'm afraid of the wardrobe room; I turn carefully down the second corridor.

Careful: if it splashes just once I'll start to wail and wail!

There are the two steps down. Push the door on the left—and I'm in the schoolroom.

Her room, Anna Amosovna's, lies farther. A sixth sense moves me to take my wailing there, beyond her screen, there onto her bed.

Who would guess that of my own free will I would come to what I ran from into hiding?

In a corner at the head of the bed, once I'd cleared away the two large pillows and covered myself with them, I felt suddenly oppressed by the enormous silence . . .

And the wailing didn't come.

But my heart was crushed, as though with a flat, broad palm. Pinched even. It seemed as if my teacher had swept her nearsighted, heavy hand across it—not across the grayish dust-mote-midge, but across my heart; it was there she had crushed the midge into a nearly invisible, incredibly tiny damp clod.

The midge had flown in to say spring had arrived, somewhere— maybe not yet in town, maybe not even where we lived in the country, but still it had arrived somewhere nearby, because if it hadn't come, then the midge in its cocoon, or wherever it slept, wouldn't have sensed it and woken up.

And once more I thought of spring. Remembering it, I had a dull sense that I loved spring and hated it, but why I loved it and why I hated it—I didn't know.

In the spring we'll go to the country, and I'll see my animals.

I have lots of them: big ones and little ones, wild ones and tame ones . . . But my thoughts grow indistinct beneath the pillow, saturated with the greasy smell of heliotrope pomade. And I don't even know now if I want to see my animals.

And is it not because of them that I hated the spring that runs and shouts, that is expansive and fragrant, that will carry me away from the stone city?

I love animals very much, but they die, and often it's just when I love them that they die.

And more than ever they die in spring; probably because more of them are born in spring. A horrible lot.

And every one that's born, who I see, I will love. I always tried to find their little eyes, and almost every one I could kiss.

And underneath the pillow I started remembering.

I remembered the little turtles. There were two of them, Titti and Totti. They had English names, because we still had an English woman living with us then. With them it was always amazing that they were stone, and suddenly out of the stone twirls a little head flat as a snake's, twisting upward, with a short little neck of leathery gathers. And little paws the same way. And the eyes in their little heads were so thoughtful and slow. If you brought them into the room they'd both start cheeping in a voice like a chick's.

I hold them by their stone backs and kiss them right on cold little mouths, stretched forward in a narrow curve, while the English woman turns fastidiously away.

"Dirty beasts!"*

She's calling clean turtles dirty beasts.

You're the one who's dirty, even though you scrub yourself with cold water winter and summer!

When they dug beneath the plank and crawled off from their fence and landed in the grove, where there are enemies, where it's cold in the fall—I cried a lot and put up two markers in the animal

* English in the original.—TRANS.

cemetery, with the inscriptions "Titti" and "Totti," just to remember them. In the fall the markers rotted and fell down. In winter the cemetery, beyond the now-ravaged flower garden, was covered with snow. That fall we hadn't yet gone into town—hurrah!—we were there for the first snow.

Once I'd remembered my turtles properly I still wasn't crying under the pillow, but suddenly the English woman's words, when I was still kissing them, came back to me clearly:

"Dirty beasts."

And I quietly started to cry.

From the very first tears, my pinched heart started to swell and I cried still harder with the pain. As if on purpose, to remember more. Like sprinkling salt on a wound.

I remembered a little fox. They had caught her alive on a hunt. They put her in the annex loft, in the workroom. Right exactly across from the one where my doves lived. I went to visit her. I took her raw meat.

The fox would steal into the far corner, wouldn't come close to the meat, and from the corner she would fasten her horrified gaze right on my eyes.

I squeeze up to the plank door, and we look at each other. It always seems to me that she wants to jump and gnaw my bare ankles with the sharp teeth she bares.

I shake all over, quite unlike me to be afraid. I want to flee, but I feel broody and can't. From a kind of heartsickness I can't.

Once the fox gnawed a crack in the plank door and disappeared.

And a sign of her flight remained: three of my rabbits—long-haired, droopy-eared, red-eyed—with gnawed out innards.

I grew quite bored of crying about animals. There were too many of them to remember.

There was the little gray rabbit. My brothers brought him back from a hunt alive. He sat in my room in a basket. Fleas ate him up.

Probably because his mother wasn't there to lick him. Or maybe because of the Persian powder I sprinkled him with, till he turned yellow?

More and more my animals crowded into my memory-heart, and for some reason my heart felt hurt, without at all knowing why or at whom, but it clearly felt hurt.

Maybe at Anna Amosovna for the midge?

No, let her get the midge . . . I don't care.

Once more, as when I'd been in the dining room with the midge, I saw our spring grove and stopped crying.

To gallop like a horse through the grove, your head far away in playful thoughts, in a land where all is freedom and heroic deeds, and easy, victorious strength—and suddenly a chirp, a quiet one, but so persistent that the most impetuous of treads stops short at it, and with one slap your heart drops to the bottom of your chest.

I stand. The chirp is nearby: there's something piteous, something greedy and too foolish in its unstoppable persistence.

I turn from the path into the grass; my feet get tangled—they're no longer hooved, they're simply ungainly, not quite sure-footed, stumbling easily in shoes that are too sturdy, made not to size but for rapid summer growth.

The chirp is beneath a tree, under a maple, not the nearest one. Farther on there, deep amid other maples, there where the grass clings and tangles, strange high grass that comes out of nowhere.

How was it audible on the path I'd left behind, from such a distance? Here it was neither louder nor quieter, it was foolish, even, greedy.

Still I'm looking for where it would be. And I find it. I bend over, disentangle a baby bird from the tangled grass that has thrust triumphantly over the rot of last year's dead leaves. He himself thrusts his breast against my hand insistently and courageously, as though swimming.

The small, dirty red body is stuck with unsightly first feathers, like gray pegs. His crop bristles, beneath the crop there's something pale blue, and beating there, beating as though on the outside, in the pale blue sack of the breast—is the heart. Stuck onto the awkward bare thread of a neck is the tiny head. It's not the head that's big, it's the beak. A heart and a beak, and then round, black little eyes. The heart beats in the sack, the beak is wide open and chirping, and the eyes stare greedy and bold like two blackish sequins in yellowish film—those eyes seem to fear nothing, understand everything, they're just demanding something, as though they're cheeping along with the yellow beak.

I bring the baby bird up to my mouth. I think he needs to be warmed. And I start to feel horribly irked. And then when he dives into my hand and sticks his beak in my mouth, this revolting thought comes suddenly to mind:

"If your teeth clinch you'll crush the beak."

How disgusting, and how tempting!

I remembered the feeling even now, under the pillow; I ground my teeth. I hadn't brushed them for a long time; they were gritty when I licked them with my tongue, after grinding them. My heart was still swollen. It didn't help to cry so quietly, inaudibly.

I needed to wail, absolutely needed to wail. Without that nothing would end. But my throat was clenched and dry, ticklish, it didn't succeed in wailing.

And then it was disgusting that the whole of that green spring, when it smells so good and summer is ahead, was spoiled by baby birds. I really wanted to cover my ears and not see or hear what I shouldn't. It wasn't my fault that my eyes were so ridiculously put together that they saw what they shouldn't and heard what they shouldn't.

There were lots of them, naked and stupid. You can't leave them in the grove to cheep—they call for their mother, but cats, moles, and rats will come running.

I'll carry them to a cage—they get swollen, their round eyes get covered with film, only wet chinks will remain, they fall stupidly to one side, twitch their yellow legs and, while I'm praying in the storeroom for their lives, they keel over.

It's so unpleasant to remember it that I try not to think; I burrow my face into the softest part of the pomaded pillow. It's stuffy, dark, hot, my nose itches . . . and I sneeze, and then listen: steps.

Have they guessed? No. Despairing of finding me, having searched all the wardrobes, they're headed here. The steps get closer. I cover myself completely with pillows and lie absolutely quiet, as though in a burrow.

The familiar flat footsteps come heavy and flat. Then quiet. Where is she? Is she standing above her bed behind the screen, has she noticed the pillows, turned topsy-turvy as though in an eruption?

Quiet . . . Silence. My heart starts beating again in my chest. Anna Amosovna would have long since tossed the pillows off me, would have long since named a punishment, would be giving her sermon now . . .

Something scrapes: the feet of the armchair moving across the floor; Anna Amosovna has moved it up to the table. Anna Amosovna is sitting in her armchair.

I move my head quietly and breathe. Pondering. What to do? I hadn't expected this. This trap.

I set to thinking, breathing freely that way. I liked it. The enemy is there. Death. Only a screen between us. I know. The enemy is unsuspecting.

The enemy is a giant. His palm is bigger than the dinner table. It's flat, rough. It'll swipe me and—I'm a spot, a damp clump, like that one . . . far away, in the dining room, from the midge.

But I'm not afraid. I'm not a fox. I'm myself. I'm not a horse. The legs are a horse. I am the head. And the horse will whisk the head away from the ogre.

For the giant is an ogre.

I feel proud-hearted. I'll sit with my head that way, curved up snake-fashion, like a turtle, and think. Suddenly I wanted to think again. I relished even the pain in my heart. But it wasn't that I wanted to think, really, I wanted to remember again.

So they all pass by, my animals—my life, my happiness and delight, and my pain at separations. I felt it, and the feel of it set off my memory . . . And there was Kellersha.

She was French—well, not really French but Swedish or Finnish—but anyway, Mama felt sorry for her and invited her for the summer. Kellersha was a teacher, well, not really a teacher, but . . . a ballerina. What a ballerina is, and why it's so funny and shameful to be a ballerina, I had no clear idea, although I felt it was funny and not quite proper.

I discovered that at Dolgovo by the sea. There was a small pond there; it went from the small grove around the house right down to the waves. Fragrant, short juicy grass grew right up to the waves, grass thick and shaggy as a bear's hide. Early in the morning there was dew on it, and skinny wild carnations like pale rose starlets.

Barefoot, I run to the sea. There's a boat in the little pond there, and I have a small bucket in my hands. I clamber into the boat and take a scoop with the bucket. The bucket is full of small fish, little ones as long as a needle, and you can see their eyes: they look slant-ways, as though in both directions. I carry the bucket home and pour the fish into the washtub. I put the tub on the windowsill on the belly-shaped balcony.

I put it there and suddenly see my sister and older brothers through the window. They've climbed up the old birches and are hiding in the broad July branches; they have laughing, sly faces that wink back and forth knowingly. They're watching something happening in the house, something funny and not quite right.

And I jump toward them, out the window right onto the steps and down under the trees, like a wobbly horse.

I scramble up a branch barely higher than the ground. I'm looking.

You have to look into Kellersha's window. The old woman is in the small room, her thin, pomaded braid wound round her rose-colored bald spot, her face podgy and swollen and reddened. She is dancing.

Up on her thin little toes she twirls, the dirty hem of her skirt lifted high, revealing emaciated chicken legs in red tights darned with white.

I see clearly from my branch.

She draws back to the near wall, with an agile, agile beadlet of a step, and her thin little body barely quivers. Then forward again, still on her tippy toes, her narrow insteps stretched straight, her leg thrust high. She doesn't fall! Her brittle old bones are all shaking, and her leg goes higher and higher, while the other one on tiptoe is taut as a string. I'm still with ecstasy and terror—not breathing, so I won't scream out "Hurrah!"

Kellersha staggers . . . she holds her arms up. I let out a suppressed cry. My brothers hiss. She doesn't hear . . . She has already clasped her hands in a light cupola above the gray head, and the heavy skirt flaps against red legs . . .

Then once more the ballerina twirls and twirls, right beside the window, only the rose-colored bald spot is shining. The braid has slipped off, untwirls like a silver snake, and the rose-colored bald spot takes turns with the rose-colored face: now the bald spot, now the face, now the bald spot, now the face, and they're both round, both merging in the rapid turnings, and I no longer know which is back and which is front, and in delight and surprise I cry out:

"Hurrah! Hurrah! Bravo! Bravo!"

Then my brothers take up my delight with a chorus of laughter . . .

Kellersha stops. Suddenly, her face toward us, her wrinkled hand sends light kisses toward us, rapid and flying from her languid, triumphantly smiling lips, old and pale.

And suddenly she fears what we cannot see—us—cries out lifeless, exhausted, aged, and falls to the floor on old knees; burying her face in the windowsill, she cries out in a cracked voice:

"Che suis pertue! . . ."

Why is she "ruined"? I didn't quite understand, though the sound of her dreadful voice, one I'd never heard, immediately convinced me of the truth of her terrible words, and I wanted to change from laughter to wailing, but the helplessly, uncontrollably laughing faces of my brothers and sister distracted me—and I also started laughing, and my heart started pounding, both malicious and joyful, and still somehow frightened.

I jumped from the branch and ran toward the balcony. I'll look at the fish. I needed it then, because it was so quiet, so tender—these little needle-sized fish, with their sticking-out, sideways eyes.

Where is the washtub? Who took it? Who took it?

And right away a dreadful thought . . . As I ran to the stairs just now, all worked up, didn't I see it, the washtub? It was lying bottom up on the sand.

I lean toward the steps, because it's damp on the worn wooden steps. Yes. That's them. Lifeless, expired fish bodies.

To the kitchen for water, then back again to pick them up.

But my fingers are rough on their gentle transparence. It's horrible to touch them.

Heavy, bad, rough. It's me, me, jumping through the window in my eagerness to laugh at Kellersha, turned over the washtub. It's me who killed them, me who smothered them. It's me! Me! It's me, bad, greedy, rough. I'm the guilty one, for everything and everybody and always.

I'm the sinful one. I'm sinful.

Nothing, nothing at all will be right.

There's no hope at all, because I'm the one, I'm the one who's sinful.

"Oh, oh, oh!"

I moaned aloud.

"I will be good. I will be good. Anna Amosovna, I will be good."

And I wailed and beat my head against the screen. And I wailed and I wailed and I wailed for my sins.

»)»» «(«(«

The Centaur-Princess

Dedicated to Georgii Chulkov *

I. Sand

Slender white columns of wood hold up the roof of a semicircular balcony. It's no longer a semicircle now: it's regular and square with a concrete floor and flat, plastered, brick pilasters. That's how my brother rebuilt it after one of the wooden columns my grandfather built rotted and fell on my sister's shoulder.

On the balcony stands a round table too big to put your arms around, laid with coffee, cream, tea, a pitcher of milk, fruit fizzes and caraway-seed buns, yeast breads and gingerbread cookies. And already there's a large fragrant plate of the first wild forest strawberries.

I must be about ten years old.

In the morning I sat, as I always did in the morning, at lessons with Anna Amosovna and felt cross, listening with melancholy yearning to the sluggish drone of a bee held captive by the ceiling, to the resonant thudding of its insistent little body on the window glass. Then we all had lunch, all the many members of our summer

* Georgii Chulkov (1879–1939) was a writer, an essayist and a critic, the author of a brief work on "mystical anarchism," and the editor of the symbolist journal *Torches,* in which both Zinovieva-Annibal and Ivanov had work published.

family, here on the balcony. Later, when Anna Amosovna went off to her room to read Plato—grumbling at the empty-headedness of youth—we all ran to the bay window to get balls and mallets and wickets, all of us: the older children and I and even Mama. We raced through the shady grove to the broad, grassy croquet field, flooded at that hour with scorching June sun.

It's hot and clear, emerald and gold, and there's a ring and buzz of unseen wings, the chirring of invisible grasshoppers.

The battle of the blues and reds takes off. I am always red and hate the blues. I'm little. I grip the long heavy mallet tightly in both hands and hit the big striped balls accurately, with incredible strength. I bring victory to the reds everywhere, and destruction to the enemies, the blues.

My older brother is a blue. My older brother is always a blue, hates the reds and gets indignant at me, sticks the upturned mallet into the turf in a fury and yells out in a choking voice:

"You devil doll!"

But I'm happy, and run happily in the scorching sun toward the home stake, skipping after my bold ball as it rolls away from its devastated enemies. And in hot, victorious snatches of thought I wonder:

"What kind of doll does the devil have?"

And try as I might, I can't imagine.

Here on the croquet field I'm a queen, young and bold. I do what I want and order others to do as I wish. No one even dares to punish me, since then I'll have a tantrum and quit the game, and, if I quit, the game will be over, and we must play for three hours: from lunch till tea, the one they've laid on the old balcony, the tea I remember even now.

But in fact, I don't know which one I remember. Probably I'm remembering lots, but since every summer there is a first time for the first wild strawberries, a first time for them to smell of sun, and once of pineapples . . . then . . . then all the times must be linked with this one in my memory.

My brothers are sitting down, as are my sister and governess—the French one, Anna Amosovna (without Plato but contemptuous); and there are guests—our neighbors—and everyone is complaining that our poor mother isn't left in peace. That's because Mama offers help, and peasants come from all around to see her.

"Why don't they see them in the office?"

"They see them there, but they want to see me personally . . . That's because when Vasya was still alive . . . we did everything ourselves . . . but now . . . you can't bury the children in the country."

Smiling shyly, disjointed words stumbling over stifled thoughts, Mama bestirs herself again and again and hurries in her unsure, awkward way to the side stairs that lead from the balcony to her favorite carpet bed of flowers. She stops by the stairs. At the bottom, on the tamped-down and sand-strewn landing, stands a peasant woman, followed by a peasant, followed in turn by more peasant men and women. What was going on? Is it a famine year, remembered along with that fragrant first wild strawberry, or did it happen that way for many years? Or were there many years of famine? Or is everything that happened many years remembered as one, as the first wild strawberries are remembered in the smell of one first berry, all untruths in one untruth?

They stand. Suddenly several of them fall to their knees on the tamped-down earth strewn with gold-colored sand. They bow low to the ground. Then Mama bows, awkwardly, stumbling a bit. She tugs and pulls at the supplicants, and with her free hand rearranges her lace headdress where it has fallen forward again and to the side.

"Bow to God! Get up! There's no need. Bow to God!"

I feel uncomfortable. It's terrible to see these sharply bent bodies on the elegant, clean sand that's so unlike the earth. And beyond the backs, over the broad, multicolored carpet of sumptuous flowers, over the golden meadow, held on two sides by stands of trees—I see the pond, shining weakly with its two islands; farther on, along the county road, a row of watchful birches by the roadside are etched in fields against pale blue. The distance stretches like a bow, a dark blue bow where the sky brushes far blue forests.

I steal quietly away. I don't eat any honey cakes. I run through the two-toned hall with the old yellow piano by the wall and the huge yellow stars on the patterned ceiling far above. I run through the front hallway, from which my favorite stairway, narrow and wooden, leads up to where we sleep; you can take it four yellow steps at a time; there are gigantic antlered mooseheads hanging on the high walls, like broad-branched tree trunks, their broad eyes looking glassily (I often dreamed of them coming to life), and a bright lamp in front of the broad porch landing—then I speed down the flat wooden entryway steps, now also cement, onto the sand-strewn entryway landing. Across from it and a bit to the left stand two old linden trees, my mother's favorites, in front of the annex with its two covered porches, one upstairs and one down. How Mama wept, wrenching, aggrieved tears—already an old woman in her second childhood—when my brother chopped down her lindens so they wouldn't cause mildew in the annex!

Directly across from the entry stands a high wall of wild roses in full bloom, and beneath it a bench—a long, bent, swinging board hung from two sawhorses. I feel like swinging. I sit down in the middle . . .

But beyond the wild roses, high, light-trunked aspens, elegant and restless, flash back and forth with their two-toned leaves, like quivering sparks in the sun.

I long to crawl up into one of them, the most comfortable one. From the next-to-the-highest branch, the crown begins to bend and I feel heavy, but you can see the sea beyond the groves and fields, the forest and still more forest. Our land goes as far as the sea, and by the sea is our village, Dolgovo. You can run barefoot there all day on white, still wet sand; you can feel the precious curves and tight ripples with the bottoms of your feet—the memory of waves that have run themselves out. You can jump barefoot there all day long on red granite boulders, rubbed smooth by the tide of the emerald gulf. I long for the top of the luminous, sunny aspen.

But even there something gets in my way . . . Either that, or memory, like a bad dream or those concave glasses, has focused all its burning rays on one point, to wound my heart with fire.

Peasants: men and women. There are peasant women beneath the lindens, and on the swing board by the wild rose there are peasant women.

Oh, of course they aren't swinging. They sit motionless, stock-still, with swaddled infants in their arms, rigid and implausible as logs . . . Then Mama is there and they are all talking. I listen to the quiet laments, flat, heavy, long and drawn-out, stirred by neither anger nor hope.

"Can't you give us pasture that's grassier and a bit closer? The cows come back at evening with no milk, they trample the crops the road's so long, and then there are fines . . ."

"The manager sent us away. He won't hear of it.

"Couldn't we rent a bit of land, either for money or for hay at harvest time? Even in a good year there's not bread enough to last halfway through Lent. The manager sows rye in all the fields near the estate, in hopes of selling it. And he's pulling out the stumps in the forest by the new pasture . . .

"He won't hear of it . . .

"Can't we get some wood for building? We burned out. We're left in the field with the shirts on our backs. The village wood is piddling and knotted. What good is it for building? The manager said, I've had a big order for lumber. Now he'll float off everything he can cut . . .

"He won't hear of it . . ."

The other one's husband has simply run her out. The husband is in town with another wife, not his real one. The children are hungry, the hut is falling down. The peasant commune took back their land. They always take it from a widow . . . If help doesn't come, *salvation*, she'll have to go off with her three and leave the fourth as a herdsman. He's already eight, almost nine.

Mama listens, her purse out. The purse is filled with silver. She gives silver to the peasant woman, and to the people who'd been burned out. She promises to talk with her eldest son about the pasture and the field.

"Only, you see . . . if the manager said so, then most likely it's truly impossible . . . of course, if it were possible . . . you see, if both peasants and masters lose their money . . . it's all economics, of course, it's all economics . . . the manager understands that better . . ."

And Mother's voice stumbles over thoughts there's no hiding from, stops short, falls silent . . .

From the porch, the house servant calls us to supper. Then I hear the lively, intermittent ring of hooves, lots of them, clattering down the lane. For a moment my heart felt joyful, for a moment it felt wild and free as it shuddered and set to pounding, stunned by the sweet clatter.

My sister galloped up with my brothers and the young folk from nearby, and jumped off her sweat-drenched horse. It breathed splendidly, wild with the interrupted rapture of the gallop.

"Mama, we're ravenous."

My dear sister's light blue eyes burn with a wild fire from her pale, thin face; her nostrils expand slightly as she breathes in.

Mama smiles in confusion. Mama loves it when we're happy. In my presence she often says to the older ones:

"Life is a terrible thing!"

And what cowed eyes she had then, consumed with horror.

"Be joyful, my children! My poor, meek children—be joyful!"

I didn't understand why we were meek, and why meager, bitter tears burst suddenly from those dark blue eyes with the large whites . . .

Over dinner, in the large dining room divided in two by high pilasters and walls of hothouse plants, I'm not friendly with the others, I don't shout hurrah at the gigantic dish of monstrous red-clawed crabs. The bloody aromatic roast beef disgusts me, and even the *varenets*—golden brown, rich, like sour cream—I don't eat.

"What's the matter with her?"

I'm silent. I'm thinking. I think: why did they make it this way? Why? Why? Why not make it some other way? Why not give it away? Why not?

"Mama, why don't we give it away?"

"Give what away?"

"Everything, everything! So it would be okay to have supper."

Mama doesn't understand. She says something . . . Then she suddenly understood and her words faltered and died away. She looks guiltily at her dear ones' faces.

But they are laughing.

"If you give away your supper you'll have no supper at all!"

They didn't understand. I burst into tears and went out.

In the evening, when I'm already nearly asleep, I hear my sister's voice and my mother, defending herself timidly:

"But what if it's made of cotton? I don't deprive you children of anything. And anyway, in other countries lots of people wear cotton underwear. It's all the same to me . . . And there will be a few extra rubles . . . for the poor. . ."

II. Forest

I got lost in the forest on purpose.

I went straight through the thicket along the edge of the bog, through meadows and clearings, keeping the sun at my left shoulder till the enticing, docile "hallooes" were no longer audible. All I heard was the rustle of falling branches, the calling of birds, the singing of treetops above.

My hat hangs on the back of my neck, dangling by its elastic band. The large heavy basket is already full, and against my stomach my knotted apron slaps like a wide pocket; it, too, billows heavy with mushrooms. My shoes and stockings are over my shoulder and my thoughts are somewhere far away, somewhere inconceivable, wandering and free. I am the princess of a wandering people. The mushrooms are my booty. I overcome all dangers and endure all kinds of exhaustion—for the booty.

There's a clearing in the wood. I will rest there, put the heavy load down.

Dense rows of aspen and birch trees surround the clearing. Soft, luxurious, flowering grass grows here; there's a ring and buzz of wild bees, and it smells of sweet honey, heady mint, and birch leaves. But one more scent mingles with the fragrances of the lazy meadow. It tickles my nose; all thoughts of rest are gone . . . I've got to keep looking, to get more.

There they are, between trunks by the roots of an aspen! An untouched, unseen treasure, blushing red. Some are so big they're like Chinese pavilions, reddish-violet. They're already old and worm-eaten. I don't hit them with my foot—it's mean. Let them be, in the open forest . . . Those others are younger, just barely out of the ground—strong little cupolas on healthy gray stalks. And then some aren't even born yet!

I dig them out with greedy fingers, and, beneath the soft damp rot of autumn leaves, I gaze in delight at tiny heads still quite rosy-yellow, on a body completely firm, not the slightest touch of fungus. These are what I smelled: these are what I tore from under autumn's rot. The princess's sense of smell is keen.

But where to put them? I tear off my hat. In a matter of minutes the hat is filled with young aspen scaberstalks.

Then, farther on, on the grass itself beside a birch, I glimpse bright auburn birch scaberstalks—golden, russet meadow mushrooms on gentle, slender white legs. I must have them, too. I can't leave them . . . but where to put them? I take off my skirt to tie up the pile I've picked. How will I carry it?

Still farther along the shore there's a smooth patch of ground.

Oh, my Lord, how many milkcaps there are! Of course I pooh-pooh them, but these are so clean—bright yellow, pale rose, violet, and purple—the yellow traceried birch leaves have clung to their brilliant skin, and they still hold fresh droplets of dew in their tiny navels. Where to put them? Oh Lord, where . . . My stockings! What's the use of them anyway? The princess has clean legs, no matter that they're brown with sun and earth. The earth is clean. And the princess doesn't wear stockings, anyway. She's been swimming in the pond and barely managed to put on her shoes and hop on the wagon.

And carefully I tuck my new treasure into one of the stockings. I keep the second for other prospects; I've already learned from the forest's abundance. I have no more thoughts of rest. It's not time for that, and, besides, my spirit has caught fire.

And there are other prospects: in the middle of the clearing three tall birches glow with the late afternoon sun; beneath the birches, of course, there are milkcaps!

I run up to them. The grass is tender and caressing, soft as velvet on weary feet unkindly pricked by windfallen branches.

And the milkcaps! Their sap is like blood—the body clean, reddish, and crackled. My stocking is full, full as the fulfillment of my wishes. My spirit is calmed by the forest's wealth, by the excess of the great, wild, willful forest, the forest that has no end . . .

I fall into warm, resinous pine needles. I roll about in them, rub my back and my scarless head, then bury my face and breathe gleefully.

I crawl along the slippery needles to the grass, like a small wild creature. Now the princess is a little beast. A fox? A little mole? A badger? Simply an animal, that special kind that a wandering princess turns into, in order to flee from humans. Because people are boring, they don't understand those who wander.

Raspberries. Wild raspberries. Wild forest raspberries! The animal princess, crawling farther, creeps up to bushes of fragrant forest raspberries. These creatures feed on forest raspberry. They stand like this on their hind paws, just as I do now, and pull off berries with their fore paws, stuffing their mouths with them.

"A-oo! A-oo! A-oo!"

I leap up, my heart pounding in fear.

Where are the voices?

Where is the sun?

Oh my God, the sun's already gone! The intense glow has already burst and faded above the green forest.

But where are they—to the left? the right?

If I stand this way, it's to the left, but if I stand this way, it's to the right.

How did I get to the clearing? I can't remember. Which way did I come out toward the clearing? Can't remember. I've gotten so turned around in the slippery needles that all directions are one. Probably I turned long ago, even before the clearing, running after booty, so that my right shoulder, instead of my left, was toward the sun, and I ended up with them close to me, still calling and calling.

"A-oo! A-oo! Vera-a-a. A-oo-oo!"

I don't answer. I don't like answering people in the forest. But still it's evening—even though the day will linger through the whole white night.

So I shuffle reluctantly toward the voices.

A bonfire smokes on the large haying field, near Devil's Marsh. The smoke keeps the flies off the horses. I trudge up to the cart, which has brought five empty linen baskets along with supper. The linen baskets are filled now and stand alongside the cart. I can barely fit in my lavish load.

The family is having supper around a second fire. They've brought last year's faded gray hay from the ricks, and my brothers and their tutor lie on it, stretched out on their stomachs. The eldest lies there, too; he's saying something to Mother in his slightly squeaky voice. My sister lies on her back, looking straight up into the pale green sleepless sky, thinking silently of something. She doesn't blink. The governess sits beside Mother. Then there's Nadya, my oldest brother's wife, with Kolyushka, still nursing, and his nanny. The fire has burned down. It's no longer smoking. The large burning embers smolder and then a film of gray ash slowly covers them.

I get scolded: why have I taken my shoes off—there are snakes. But I like snakes. They won't bother me.

I can see that Mother's upset about something. My older brother finishes what he was saying when he got interrupted.

"If you don't levy taxes on mushrooms and berries, the people will lose respect for property even more. Why shouldn't they chop down the forest on an estate then? Why not just steal our wheat once they've eaten up their own? You'll not help the people with crumbs like that. The corruption of historical principles leads them to their ruin . . ."

"Mama, are mushrooms and berries property?"

I put the question, stupidly surprised.

That means the wandering princess was stealing mushrooms when she took booty for her camp? And the strange beast eating raspberries—was that stealing too? How wonderful—why doesn't everyone steal? Then it all would belong to everyone . . . If everyone up and started stealing? . . .

We're already in the big wagons, coming out onto the edge of the forest over the marshy ruts of the woodland road. Something like dusk has settled on the dense woods. Suddenly I long fiercely for the dark of night and sleep.

We stopped at a cottage by the forest's edge. The young people wanted to have some sour kvass, the village kind. In the fresh air it was much tastier than the bottled kvass on our estate, which was sweet and thick and bubbly. The old man brought out a wooden jug. I followed Mama into the low, sooty cottage.

A chimneyless smudge-lamp gave off smoke. An elderly woman lay groaning on the sitting ledge. Beside her in the cradle lay a filthy rag, and a nauseating sour smell assaulted my nose. My eyes kept me bent over, though, despite the smell. Sooty shadows jumped along the yellow skin of an old-one-child, a child-skeleton; they jumped along hands much too long, finger-spiders with tiny bodies on long, tiny paws that moved quietly and fantastically above the skull-head, grasping and picking with pawlike fingers at sinuous shadows of smudge.

Mama asks questions. The woman is sick; she's exhausted herself: something in her stomach has split. And the child is from the foundling home.

"Are you nursing?"

"Good Lord, how could that be! My husband's been gone for two years with no word."

"Do you have a cow?"

"Mother, good lady, her milk went bad, I sold her to the butcher this winter, right before the Holy Days. Our own wheat didn't last even till Epiphany. I've no idea how I'll make do now . . . And plus I've no notion how to get the farm work done. I feed the old one bread still—now listen, kind lady, don't tell the doctor about it. If he finds out he'll take him away. They give me three rubles at the foundling home; I've got four of my own!"

The old woman moaned.

"But with you he's not long for this world."

"True enough, dear lady. He's exhausted me. When he came to me he was sick. Dear God. What cares I haven't had with him. Now he won't let me get a rest. I take better care of him than I did my own . . ."

I begin to grow accustomed to the old one in the cradle, to seeing him.

"Mommy, Mommy, it's a little boy just like our little Kolya, only he's so skinny. Mommy, Mommy—Nadya has milk in her breasts. Yesterday she used a pump to squeeze it out. Half a glass."

"Now, now. It's time to head home. They're calling us. It's late for Kolya to be out. Nadya will be worried."

"Mama, tell her we'll take this one home. Nadya can feed him, too."

"That's stupid. He might have a disease. We don't know the parents. How can we do that?"

Blushing, Mama takes her purse awkwardly; the silver clinks rapidly in her fingers.

"Here, here . . . buy him some milk. And . . . I'll send you some special oil to rub your belly."

III. The Crop-Eared Roan Horse

Already it's early summer once again. Because the grasses are high, and in flower.

Already I'm older, because I feel like a wandering princess less often; sometimes in moments of un-selfconsciousness—but then all the more passionately, and with an insistent melancholy.

I stand on the high bank of the ditch that marks the edge of our park grove, looking into the distance.

There in the distance lies the sea. Beyond the fields, beyond the woods, and still farther beyond fields and woods lies the sea. If only I could run that far! Run and run until I'm there. There's a small boat there. There are gray boats there among the reeds, fishermen's. I don't like the painted ones that belong to our estate; they're too heavy. I want to sit in a fishing boat and shove off from the shore with a pole. At first it will scrape bottom on the sand below and knock against the round boulders beneath the water. Then it will rock, rock free, and—I'm off. I'll take the oars and row quietly. I steer a secret passage, a familiar one, between gigantic underwater cliffs—there are two tricky ridges—right out into open water. Broad, flat rolling waves run between them: they lap and cover them, then thrust back, foaming fiercely. For a moment they uncover the red and yellow granite backs and then roll on, jagged and disheveled, toward offshore shoals. Beyond the ridges in the open sea lies an expanse that is mine, a path in all directions. A small sail lies on the deck. I hoist it with the tow-rope onto a high pole in the middle of the boat, then thread the sheet through a block to the stern. I sit at the tiller. The wind has touched the sail. The sail luffs and yields. It's curved like a rocking cradle; the boat has heaved to. There it is—the distance, where sky has touched the sea—stretched like a broad, pliant shaft-bow, bent like a tautened bow. Into the distance! Into the distance! All paths lead there. For there are no boundaries to the sea: the sea is a path; the sea is all paths.

There was a whinnying noise quite close, and I jumped down and let out a cry. From behind the trunk of an old birch in the field to my left, I see a roan muzzle poking out from a broad peasant shaft-bow; there are dark brown spots over large, golden-hazel eyes. The golden equine eyes watch me attentively, un-blinking, staring their utterly animal stare, gentle and unyielding. From somewhere in the grass nearby comes laughter—and then it halts abruptly.

I see her, the girl in the ditch who had laughed, standing in the high, flowering grass, and I step angrily toward her. She jumps up straight like a boy, slender and steady, with a face like the roan horse's, dusky as the barely warmed skim on rich baked cream. Golden-hazel eyes stare from that small roan face into my angered one—unrelenting, unblinking, without either hope or fear. Only the full lips, the deep red of overripe wild strawberries, quiver slightly.

We measure each other up with our stares, and suddenly I have a vision of that distance, the shaft of the taut bow. My anger passes, and there's a rumbling in my ears like sea foam, like the fine silver bubbles of sweet wine . . .

"What were you laughing at?"

Against my will the words come out affectionate and cheerful.

"You frightened Chalko, and he whinnied."

"What's your name?"

"Tanya."

"What are you doing here?"

"Nothing . . . I'm waiting for my pa to come back from the estate office."

"Have you been waiting long?"

Tanya looks toward the west. You can already look straight into the sun. It's getting toward evening.

"He left this morning."

"Do you live far from here?"

"We're from Zabolotye."

"Have you eaten?"

"Nuh-uh. And Chalko's hungry."

"Let's tear off some grass for him."

"I've already done that."

"Well, let's do it together."

We tear juicy grass from the ditch. I crawl on my knees; my knees and hands are both green. The grass in the ditch is very juicy. Chalko eats and blinks his hazel eyes. The red sun catches him straight in his large eyes; the deep, deep eyes shine through with gold. We've unharnessed him and he chomps on the grass; we've put a whole pile in front of his nose. He's young, his nostrils are delicate and quiver eagerly. His forelock and mane are like Tanya's hair: brown, lit up in the sun like dark honey.

"Chalko suits you, Tanya; he looks like you."

"I look like my pa. And roan horses suit everybody. He's not raven-colored."

"Tanya, what's the matter with his ear?"

"He's crop-eared."

"How come?"

"Last summer, when he was a colt, he fought with one of the horses in the herd."

"He's a troublemaker."

"He's got a heart like mine, won't give in."

Tanya laughs and her white teeth show.

"Only his teeth aren't like yours."

I look at his young yellow teeth with their unworn black hummocks; I pry open his rose-colored, whinnying jaw.

I remember that Tanya hasn't eaten either.

"Are you hungry?"

"Mama didn't have bread this morning."

"Why not?"

"We ate it all up yesterday. My dad went to your estate office for flour. He was going to hire out for the haying on your land. But I don't know if they'll give it ahead . . . Lord knows pa would pay it all off. He's great at haying. He's the best in Zabolotye, Lord knows."

I listen to her and think it over. It's the time of day when you'll not find anything good to eat. They'll be finishing up cooking and laying the table for supper; the serving man and cook are both hard-hearted, and the dishwashers and kitchen girls are too exhausted even to complain.

All the same, I scramble off straight through the thick grove of trees, my eyes on the fleeting whiteness of the balcony's semicircle of columns. My feelings are unpleasant and vaguely shameful; I keep driving them away. Slapping my thighs with my palm and clicking my tongue, I imagine myself a horse and my palm a whip. There's no time now to tear off a branch.

I go stealthily down the flagstone stairs to the kitchen. The kitchen is in the basement of the large old house.

It's a wandering princess, come galloping to where there are people—enemies of the wild and free. Strictly speaking, the wandering princess isn't human; but she also isn't a horse. She is half-horse, half-human. I had read about it not long before, about centaurs and how they lived in Greece. And I grasped what kind of creature the wandering princess was—a young centaur, a little centaur. Almost like Chalko, and almost like Tanya.

In mortal danger now I steal into the terrible palace, mysterious and still, to steal food for the herd. The white cook with his reddened nape stands by the stove, shaking a large frying pan in which fish blushes red, sizzling and spitting. Sweat trickles down the three tight folds in the back of his neck. The dishwasher snuffles and has to leave her wet nose unwiped, as she tears feathers from the headless corpse of a chicken still shuddering with life.

"What good is it with no head? It's not game—it's a chicken. She's scratched it off, the bitch."

Still others are pounding and hurling viciously amid the sizzle and smoke. They don't see me. There's a large crust of rye bread at the table's edge.

I grab it.

The princess has her booty. The princess will gallop away. Oh, how these young centaurs can gallop over stairways, stone ones and wooden ones . . .

I hear someone in pursuit . . . but the centaur-princess is already out of range; she's already off at full gallop through the grove, maneuvering her long body easily among dense trunks. A wandering centaur is nimble, like a snake.

There are Tanya and Chalko. I wave the crust to Tanya where she stands in the grass.

The grass at the edge of the ditch comes up to my waist. Bluebells sway violet-blue; buttercups shine rich yellow; the rose-colored clover smells of honey, and fluffy buttercup roses nod toward us under the weight of their own aroma. Great silver spiderweb spheres of dandelions shoot up above our heads. Wild sweet pea has entangled everything; it's twined everywhere, entwined everything with its strong whiskers, beside the sharp teeth of lilies that laugh out at us from the grassy thicket.

We sit and chew the fresh, fragrant rye bread in silence. The field flowers' honey seems to pour into our mouths with the bread, as though we're spooning fragrant honey with the bread.

We eat, and again look each other in the eyes . . . but this time with tenderness and confidence, sheltered above by the tall stems of delicate grasses; their golden-violet feather tassels tickle and stroke our foreheads. We've eaten our fill, and the fluffy tassels' ticklish languor flows through our bodies and glitters moistly in my Tanya's eyes.

She looks at me, and suddenly her hands wind round my neck, and her dark lips, red as wild strawberries ripened in the sun, press gently and full on my lips. And suddenly a new, unexperienced feeling shuddered in my heart and mind, each drop of blood, each vein throbbing with vital life, and the grasses and flowers parted like sea reeds when a boat clears a shoal and sets off. Close, unmoving, I saw Tanya's gaze: gentle and unyielding as if it were not human, her golden-hazel eyes unblinking. There was neither fear nor hope in them. I saw only her eyes, utterly close—and we sailed by the bluebells and the crow's foot, the buttercups and the dandelions and the tight spiral whiskers of the wild sweet pea; and all the while the high, bending grasses brushed our foreheads with soft, feathery tassels, sprinkling dry, sweet-smelling dust. Was it that, or the sweet-smelling wind that touched and tickled us, wafting honey and cool mint? Or a dragonfly that lighted on my brow, with its long, narrow, honey-blue body?

We lie together now on our backs in the grass, and it seems to me that we look through the translucent rainbow wings of my dragonfly—motionless and dimly visible above our eyes—toward the deep blue-green of the twilight sky. The sun hasn't set yet; it shines through the grass stems, and the stems throw narrow shadows, intertwined and intermittent, on other stems. A heavy green beetle crawls along a blade of grass, its festive moustache bending; the blade bends, and the beetle falls heavily on my bare flexed knee. I shudder and laugh. How thin Tanya is! What an angular body! She makes me think of Petya, a cousin who I sometimes play wild horses with.

A bumbling bumblebee, all velvety, almost plush, buzzes fat and festive by a head of lush honey clover.

"What a fine gentleman!" says Tanya, stretching her blackened, calloused hand toward the flower. "He won't bite!" and she's already sucking sweet liquid from the clover stalks, chattering all the while: "mind now! the honeybee's littler, don't touch it, it'll sting!"

"Tanya, have you been to the sea?"

We stand holding hands and look toward the sea, where the sun has sunk and dissolved in a glittering band at earth's edge.

"Un-uh. Is the sea big?"

"Big. Without end."

"And what if you sailed and sailed on a boat?"

"You could sail a long way."

"To the edge?"

"You can't sail to the edge. It starts again where it ends, because the earth is round, like a ball."

Tanya doesn't understand.

"Well, I'd just keep sailing. Sailing on. I'd sail far away. Is there more land far away?"

"There is."

Tanya's eyes burn with a kind of fire, resolute and full. Like the eyes of a horse at full gallop as it overtakes another horse. I know it myself when I gallop; when I'm a centaur, even when I'm alone, I feel that same fire. It doesn't relent; it has no need of hope.

"Tanya, there's a bit of bread left, for the horse."

And suddenly I remember that at home, at Tanya's in Zabolotye, there has been no bread since yesterday, that her mother and the other children have been waiting since morning . . . But Tanya doesn't stint. She takes the bread on her thin, flat palm and offers it in chunks to the roan horse.

"Tanya! Tanya!"

My heart flinched again, at the menacing voice, and I started back from my friend. The centaur leaped over the ditch and looked from the grove out onto the road. A peasant man came up, put on Chalko's bridle and turned, grumbling peevishly. Subdued and pale, Tanya listened and pursed her dark red lips.

And I heard words I didn't know, words that cursed and sullied, words meant for me and my family. Hatred pounded heavy at my heart, and shame, clear and aching now, swam slowly through my blood, pressing painfully on every vein in my body.

Chalko carried the peasant and his daughter calmly away, to their hungry house in Zabolotye, ten versts away . . .

And I stood for a long time, as though pierced with shame . . .

Then I slip down to the birch trunk to gather my thoughts. What exactly had happened? But I can't understand a thing. The three of us had eaten bread together: she and Chalko and me . . . then she kissed me, and it was as though a great, unknown love had come out of nowhere, and now she had left, and once again I was with them, with my own people . . . Her father's curses and abuse bound me to them, irrevocably. But I didn't feel sorry for Tanya or horror at my own family. After all, I wasn't quite a girl. Of course, I was a girl by age and birth, but then I was a centaur, too.

I remember how wildly the thought struck me, the first of childhood's resounding intuitions to claim my mind.

But it was true—truly I was, and am, a centaur. Centaurs don't know how to love their fathers' houses, with their balconies and kitchens and heads of dead moose; they don't remember their mothers and brothers, don't know how to measure land and hire men at haying time. Centaurs need what is necessary, nothing more: freedom, and a meadow. Centaurs feel sorry for no one. If they meet someone dear, they love them and are happy, but they don't cry over them, because centaurs don't know how to cry, and then too, there's much that is dear on the great, unstinting earth. All of it is loved by the centaurs, wandering and free; it belongs both to them and to others.

So, was it on that evening that it all came clear? Or was it just on that evening that the seed of clarity was sown? In any case, I discovered then, and did not forget, that by some miracle a centaur-princess, rather than a girl, had been born to humans.

And she would leave them, of course, in order to find another life.

»»» «««

The Devil

*Dedicated to Konstantin Andreevich Somov**

I. Rebellion

I was saying prayers with Mama at her icon stand, beneath her icons, as always, when she ran in to say good-night and give me her blessing.

First:

"God bless and keep Mama and Papa, Grandpa and Grandma, my aunts and uncles, brothers and sisters (my cousins, that is), then my real brothers and sisters each by name, and help me to be a good girl."

Then the Lord's Prayer and the Prayer to the Blessed Virgin.

I wasn't thinking about my prayers, and my heart started a kind of unpleasant pounding.

Mama blessed me hurriedly. The older ones were waiting for her in the troika. She kissed me, not the way she sometimes did, but hurriedly, and then ran out like a young girl. And I lay down. Everything grew distant and unreal. God, and Mama.

---

* Konstantin Andreevich Somov (1869–1939) was an artist associated with the "World of Art" movement whose sensuous paintings frequently treat erotic themes reminiscent of the eighteenth century. He was also a frequent visitor to the Tower.

I didn't feel like sleeping, because suddenly I felt bored. Probably because I'd prayed badly. I kneel in bed. No, that's lazy: I need to get on the floor by the icon stand.

It's scary.

The flame in the icon lamp barely quivers. Shadows tremble. I step shuddering along the parquet floor. I kneel down. I pray.

Elsewhere in distant rooms there is noise, bustle, preparations. Again:

"God bless and keep Mama, Papa, Grandpa, Grandma . . . ," etc.

No . . . by Grandpa I had already stopped thinking.

Again:

"Grandpa, Grandma . . . Grandma, Grandma . . . my aunts . . ."

Which ones? I don't like Aunt Klavdia. She's not honest. Anyway:

"And forgive us our trespasses, as we forgive those who trespass against us . . . forgive those who trespass against us."

That means to forgive those who hurt us. She complains about me to Mama, and puts on airs in front of me . . . and she doesn't like me or Mama . . .

Bad thoughts. I begin to shiver. It's cold and there's a rustling noise somewhere.

Oh, that awful Mlle Mokhova! Yesterday Burkovich wrote a note: "Mlle Mokhova has a booger in her nose!"

Disgusting. The piece of paper was on my desk when Mlle Mokhova walked by. I said I had written it. All the girls thought I was a hero. Mlle Mokhova assigned me two hours of copying. Tanya was waiting in the entrance hall at school, in a temper, and took me home. Mokhova had given her a note of complaint for Mama. At home Mama sent me right to bed, without letting me play with Volodya and without having said good-night.

Yesterday Burkovich cried through the whole first lesson, head down on the desk. We were sitting together. When she lifted her head, there was a puddle on the desk from her eyes and nose. Her ruddy face was spotted red, her eyes with their heavy lashless lids were all swollen. I comforted her and kissed her in spite of myself, because everyone hates her for being dirty; it made me feel sick, but I wanted to spite everyone.

"And keep me from temptation . . ."

How did I get here? . . . And what about before? Did I think or not? . . .

Early tomorrow to school for the whole day again, till eight o'clock. Boring.

"Our Father . . ."

There are footsteps coming down the hallway. My sister runs into the room. I'm already in bed and keep quiet. Had Sister forgotten something . . . or is it for Mama? She feels around and finds it in the half-dark, then runs to the illuminated doorway . . .

It's wonderful in a troika. They're having fun, and Mama is theirs. And I'm the only one who has to get up tomorrow at seven, when Tanya whispers so as not to wake my sister, and takes me off . . . to the far-off classroom, where my washstand is, where earlier, before this horrid school, I took lessons with Anna Ivanovna, and before that with Anna Aleksandrovna, and before that with Katerina Petrovna, and before that . . .

None of them wanted to teach me anymore. One after another they refused, because I put on airs and teased.

"God bless and keep Mama, Papa . . ."

Still, I have to finish my prayers.

Do I love Papa? Papa's almost never home . . . I'm afraid of him and I don't like the way he smells. I love Mama.

There's Miss Maud* in the corridor. I made her so angry today when I was getting undressed—and she was in a hurry—that she

---

* English in the original.—TRANS.

started to cry. English women rarely cry and are very patient. Even Anna Aleksandrovna, when I intentionally drew a crooked line during drawing lesson, would sigh:

"No, with her you need English patience."

Although Volodya insists she said angelic. But I'm not sure. Volodya is two years younger than me. How could he know better than me? And anyway . . .

There are her footsteps again, and a jingling of keys. She was clearing away the tea and cookies. In winter she keeps house since I've gone to school as a full-day student . . . She hates housekeeping, and is always bad-tempered in winter. Thank God that Emma Yakovlevna is housekeeper in the summer.

"Miss Maud! I'll be good! Miss Maud! Miss Maud! I'll be good! I'll be good! I'll be good!"*

It's true, I want to be a good girl. She doesn't believe me and doesn't respond. When I make promises no one responds, because no one believes me.

"Help me be good!"

And suddenly I pray fervently, and God hears me.

If only I could stay home. If only I didn't have to go to school. That school is stupid, boring . . .

Miss Maud's footsteps.

"Miss Maud! Miss Maud! Good-night! Good-night!"

She's silent. She's closer . . .

I call out louder, howling:

"Miss Maud! Good-night! Good-night! I'll be good!"

The footsteps shuffle by, and I hear Miss Maud snorting angrily. Once more, with all my strength, sobbing:

"Miss Maud! Miss Maud! I'll be good! I'll be good!"

She doesn't believe me. Doesn't believe me. And of course I

* English in the original.—TRANS.

won't be good. It's completely impossible. For me it's impossible. Better to die. I want to jump into the hallway and bite the old red-cheeked Englishwoman.

The whole house is quiet. Of course; everyone has left. And Miss Maud will go to bed before they get home. Then everyone will drink tea again in the dining room . . . Then they'll go to bed, and soon I'll be getting up for school already. Then all day in school, and in the evening to sleep.

And again. And again.

Why doesn't Mama know how much I hate school? And what's the point of praying anyway, if it doesn't help?

I lifted my head and saw the icon lamp. It was going out: it dimmed and shuddered, then the fire leaped up with a red tongue, a red tongue, and it went out, and then the tongue jumped up again. And I stuck my tongue out at it, at the icon stand, and with a shout started thrashing about, sobbing, alone there in my bed.

In the long, narrow room there are two rows of sliding drawers along the walls. Each drawer has a key, and each day girl has her own key.

I kneel by my drawer, crying quietly . . . It's that way every morning.

The full-day girls come earlier than the others. They go over their lessons. They say prayers separately.

I would rather be a half-day student. They're free. They come and go, and have their own breakfast in little baskets. And they have a good time at home. But we come from morning till night. We're only home to sleep. You come home and go to bed alone, and Mama isn't always even home to say good-night . . .

It's still dark in the long, narrow room. The lamps are lit. Outdoors there was rain instead of snow, and it was cold and boring just now.

How frozen and raw I'd become! And tears fell like drops of bit-

ter rain, and my heart grew taut in my chest like a little lump, an icy
little lump.

In she comes, Mokhova. And tenderly, yesterday's note forgotten,
because she's very absentminded:

"Why are you crying?"

"Me? . . . My leg hurts."

"Your leg?"

"My knee."

"Did you bruise it?"

"Yes, on the bottom drawer."

Of course I can't say I'm crying because I hate school. It's awkward
somehow to say it, and I'm glad I know how to lie . . . and I'm
surprised, why did I lie all of a sudden, just like that?

The large recreation hall is empty. Rows of chairs are squeezed
onto the platform that for some reason stands there. I climb in
among them and grind my teeth on one of the backs, staring with
my sharp farsighted eyes down the endless length of empty room.
There, on the far wall, hangs a round clock, and the hand crawls
slowly along the clock face. I watch it with my unpleasantly vigilant, unhealthily vigilant eyes, how it falls, falls with brutal jerks,
from minute to minute. Is that really how minute hands move? I
thought the minutes were all together.

And I ponder:

"Where is the dust from? From the backs of the chairs or from
my unbrushed, scruffy teeth?"

Shultz! Shultz!

She sits to my right on the other side of the narrow aisle between
the school desks, in the same row as I do. She has a face that's white
and rosy, blond hair and a little blue hair comb. She has a rose-
colored little apron on, and it's pinned at the bodice to her narrow
chest. She's neat, she's German, the daughter of Baker Shultz.

I pretended that I loved her a lot. For nobody likes her, since she's the daughter of Shultz the baker, who sends us his buns for sale during recess.

Burkovich says Shultz has lice in her hair. But she just says that because she's jealous, because I gave Shultz my old soap-bubble pipe. I told Burkovich I'd bought it specially in a toy store.

I love to lie. More and more. There's something enticing about it; you never know where it will lead and what will come of it.

Shultz went out first at recess. The next lesson is German translation.

There's her notebook. Glossy blue paper. It's open. A pale blue sheet of blotting paper inside, fastened to a white ribbon with a large bouquet of forget-me-nots. My eyes fasten on the light blue bouquet on the light blue page.

I didn't move. Burkovich pulled on my hand, but I got angry.

"I'm not going."

"Then who will I go with? They're all together. I'm by myself."

"That means you deserve it."

Burkovich gets angry and leaves.

I get up. Look around. The class is empty. I grab the notebook with the forget-me-nots. I dig my scratchpad out of my desk. I shove the glossy blue-papered notebook into it and tear out of the room, down the long corridor, then through the whole recreation hall. I dive in among the pairs, threes and fours of tenderly woven friends, run farther, to the long room with the sliding drawers—and in mine, I lock my prisoner with the forget-me-not bouquet.

Everyone is assembled for German translation class. And Shultz is digging in her desk, reddening, getting worked up and already crying. I sit down beside her and together we go through her clean little notebooks and her sturdy, unstained little books.

"There it is. There it is!"

"No, no, that's not it. I left it on the desk. It was ready . . ."

"That can't be: you forgot it at home! Look, look, farther in on the right there's something."

The teacher comes in, and Shultz, sobbing, sits in her place . . .

"Bring the notebook to the next lesson. If you can't find the old one, then translate the last twelve paragraphs for me in a new notebook."

That night at home Mama didn't come to prayers. She had gone out for dinner. That whole day I didn't see her.

Next morning in school I took the shiny blue notebook out of my drawer and spent a long time tearing it up, page by page.

How clearly and evenly that clever Shultz wrote! Letter by letter. I tore the clean, smooth pages to shreds. The pale blue blotting paper with its ribbon and picture I kept, and in a week I had already attached it to my penmanship book.

Shultz saw it. Looking at me with frightened, quite startled eyes, Shultz mumbled:

"That's mine . . . that's my *klakspapir.* That's from my notebook . . . How ever—"

"Your father made meringues of it!"

Shultz was surprised by my voice, loud enough for the whole class to hear, and by my impudent proud look. She's silent. She actually believes the marvelous double in my notebook.

And the class is laughing:

"Shultz, bring us some pasties made of your notebook. Shultz, Shultz."

"Shultz, you've insulted me. Give me your blue hair comb!"

I speak sharply, above all the cries.

Frightened, Shultz unfastens the round comb from her blond, pomaded hair. I take it and break it into pieces. I fling them far away.

Today is Sunday, and at last I can play with Volodya in the nursery. But not before church.

I wander idly'from corner to corner in the hallway. In the school-room I play with my Bobik, a yellow canary with a broken leg. He jumps on my head, on my finger, bites a rusk from my lips . . .

Mama always cries in church. In church my back always hurts. I have to ask God for forgiveness all the time for not praying and for never having time to pray. When the priest comes out and after "Go in peace" says "In the name of the Father" and reads from the book—quickly, fearfully I set about making up for lost time . . . but even then . . .

We all leave church sad, because Mama is sad. Mama lives for us. But Mama is grieving. And we know that.

The Sunday pie is boring, because Mama's eyes are tearstained and her smile is timid.

Father isn't even eating with us today, so it's very quiet and list-less, and there's nothing for me to get surprised at.

But finally lunch is over, and Brother and I are in his nursery.

A large table, covered with oil cloth, pulled up with its narrow end to the wall. That's just the coach, along with our traveling house—for me it's a coachman's, for Volodya a conductor's. The real carriage is on the other side of the wall. There's a whole wagon on the other side of the wall, where dozens of people can fit. Of course I don't see them, but the conductor often has to fight with them. Then he sits with his nose to the wall and makes up whole frantic scenes in words and gestures. Of course it's hard for him, over such a long, weeks-long, trip, to deal with almost a whole nation of people that we're transporting on these twenty horses. But since he's firm-tempered, he always wants to be con-ductor again.

The chair-horses are all turned backs-heads forward, all cleverly hitched to the table legs, and in my hands are a whole pack of rope reins, cleverly threaded, and a thick coachman's whip with a long rope, tied to the end of a belt.

Volodya wears a yellow buckram jacket, and on his chest there's a sooty lantern that smells of paint.

It's a merry game. You put heart and soul into it.

What horrors are met with on wild mountain roads, where you sometimes have to cross streams, rigging boards beneath the house and setting the horses into the ford. Or several days running you drive underground through the bottomless depths of mountain tunnels. Or you encounter savages. Or the road is washed out by storms . . . Or horses get sick or die, or the passengers mutiny and you have to settle it, or . . .

It's getting on toward evening. It's getting dark. Soon, soon they'll call us to dinner.

On Sundays, we all have dinner downstairs at Grandfather's. It's different but always the same, just like the carriage carrying a whole people.

At Grandfather's we're a school. Volodya's a boy, I'm a girl, but a princess. I'm the kind of girl that all the boys recognize as the bravest and most beautiful of all, and I'm their princess. Volodya is Charlie. I'm Lucy. Grandfather is an old general who has invited the school to visit.

Grandfather has tasty dinners, because, in addition to the fourth dessert course, sometimes there's something sweet for the second course, too. Something soft with rum custard.

We children, the school, sit at the very bottom of the table. Not far from us is our disgusting cousin, the son of Aunt Clavdia. He hates me and keeps an eye out for ways to tease me.

Strictly speaking, he's not my cousin but a student from another school, our enemies', whom we disdain. I tell Volodya—he always believes me and goes along—that Mister Charlie, the director, punished our comrade Jack and locked him up in a room with bones. That's the lockup at our school. (My schoolroom, of course.) Human bones are buried in the walls there. But in the middle of the story I jump up and tell Volodya that Andrew, that insufferable joker, has crawled under the table again and is pinching me on the leg.

"Why are you jumping, fidget? Did Miss Maud put a pin in your skirt to punish your mischief?" my cousin teases.

"She's not even here. On Sundays she's always at her church."

"After church you were bad and she punished you."

"After church she goes to see friends. And you're an idiot."

My cousin turns red and shuts up, stunned by my impudence. He can only mutter.

"You just wait."

We turn down the pointless main course and wait for the fourth. I tell Charlie how Lucy—that's me—how she and Gerald took first place in a race on one and a half legs.

"Everyone ran on one and a half legs?"

"Well, yes, because all the children were tied together at the leg, so it comes out that each pair has three legs. And if you divide three by two how much do you get? Well? Or haven't you gotten to one and a half yet with Ivan Ivanovich?"

Andrew is under the table again. And I start to yell and jump around.

"Aha, that's how you behave! Aunt! Aunt!"

And over the evenly humming voices of aunts and uncles, all placed according to seniority at the head of the table with my kind grandfather and my proper grandmother—my enemy, bent on revenge, calls Mama, my mama, and everyone stops talking. I sit blushing, sick with horror.

"Aunt, you should send Vera out. She's being naughty and horsing around!"

Mama's ashamed; she blushes, too.

"Vera, what is this about?"

I say nothing.

"What are you doing?"

"There's a little boy under the table!" Volodya cries out in tears.

"That's ridiculous. It's all her stupid games," announces the enemy. "She's gone mad with them. She sees little boys everywhere."

My cousins burst into cheerful laughter.

"Vera, get up from under the table."

"What's going on there?" my grandfather asks, his voice weak in the general uproar.

"Vera has been naughty again. She's making Mama upset," Grandmother announces severely.

"Tsk, tsk, tsk, little Vera. Come here."

Everyone looks at me, and I can't move. Horrified, Volodya nudges me.

"Go to Grandfather."

Oh, I would follow Grandfather anywhere! Every Sunday when we say good-bye Grandfather himself stands up, and, leaning on his ancient cane with the ivory handle, tapping gently on the parquet floor with the rubber tip, he leads Volodya and me down the whole long hall to his study, where there's a small glassed-in covered balcony—sticking out like a belly above the street. There, every Sunday, Grandfather takes two round chocolate gingerbreads with candied fruit peel on the bottom from a box on the floor and gives us one each.

"That's for the two of you. Be good for your mama."

His old, soft voice shook and so did his kind gray head, with its small, round, wrinkled little face.

I'm always happy to follow Grandfather, and it's not even because of the gingerbread, but because of *how* he gives it to us. He's so wonderfully kind.

But now, now! . . . How can I budge, with the enemy's eyes fixed triumphantly on me? And how can I walk the length of the dining room, down the long row of aunts, uncles, and cousins? Everyone,

everyone is looking at me, and lots of them are laughing, and they're all thinking one thing:

"She's upset her mother again."

I stand there.

Grandfather is flustered. He calls my name again.

I stand there.

My eyes jump from one face to another, and my teeth chatter. Suddenly I feel my face and, at the same time, Mama's voice, like a stranger's:

"Fedya, take her out."

And Fedya, the enemy, grabs me by the shoulders and takes me out. I walk as in a dream, at someone else's will.

There's the entry hall. He's still leading me and giggling about something. I go without protest.

There's the dark corridor, and in the dark I come to myself.

I start to bellow wildly, turn suddenly, and throw myself at him. I grab him by the knees. I beat his body with the ends of my shoes and my fists. I aim my feet at his shin bones, my fists at his stomach.

And I pound like a fury, plunging my teeth into his resisting hands.

He calls out for help. Someone else is here. It looks like Grandfather's old servant.

Together, they shove me in somewhere.

And it's dark.

It's the closet where they keep things to be thrown out. In our games the Devil lives there; when we play horses in that hallway after dinner, we always go by the Devil's closet at a gallop. The coachman yells, and the horse neighs for all he's worth.

But now I don't care. I sit on the floor, just where they left me, not crying. I look through one of the cracks. It seems I don't even blink. The light through the crack is weak.

What are light and darkness to me? Everything's finished, everything's finished. And I'll die. Grandfather, I offended Grandfather.

I shamed Mama. And they can never forgive me. Nor should they forgive me. I knew, I had always known it would be my fate to die this way, in this closet with the old, broken things; that's why I feared it and neighed in a wild, high voice as I galloped by.

It's clear that I have to die, because it's quite clear that I can never reform myself, and . . . if you think like that, just like that, with your lips pressed tight and your brow knit, looking without blinking straight through the crack in the wall, if you think it through to the end, you'll discover there's no point in reforming yourself.

And anyway, I don't want to reform myself. I want the exact opposite. So when somebody's neatly dressed, with their hair nicely done, you tear their clothes off and mess up their hair. And if someone's weak, make him hurt, and then hurt some more and still more, till he squeals, till he's dead: the way they smothered a rat once in the pantry . . . So your stockings stick out of dirty shoes, the way I came home from the pond, last autumn.

And now I want to run quietly into the dining room, slip under the table, and pull on the tablecloth hard so that all the plates, the glasses, bottles, and forks would fly to the floor, so everyone would start yelling and Mama would start crying, and Grandmother would start shaking her finger at somebody or other, and Grandfather . . . I feel sorry for Grandfather, but Grandfather didn't defend me . . . And then I would jump out from under the table and bang on the wall as hard as I could.

Like Samson.

The wall would sway, it would start to rock and fall to the street, the ceiling would fall, everyone would start screaming and run out, and Fedya would be killed. But I would save Grandfather, and God would forgive me.

If you hold your breath for a long time, you'll die.

Who's that laughing? What is that? There's a quiet creak in the darkness. Suddenly I'm scared. I'm seeing things. Or is it the Devil that lives there?

If I hold my breath for a long time I'll die, and then I won't have to hear that horrible creaking anymore.

But if you die here, then you'll definitely go straight to the Devil.

What if I run away? After all, Fedya hadn't locked the door. He didn't dare. Should I try it? Why sit here like someone being punished?

Shame. Shame. How can I face everyone now? I can't bear for them to see me now. How can I run away, without anyone seeing me?

I touch the door quietly. It gives. I stick my head out. After the closet, the corridor seems light.

And the light is more frightening than the darkness. I know that for sure now. I close the door. The Devil creaks in the closet, but I like it. It's nice because it's dark. I'm not ashamed of the Devil. The Devil himself does everything like me. And God drove the Devil out, too, like from under the table. That means that he and I are comrades. We both don't want to be good; we've both been driven out.

And it isn't scary . . .

After New Year's I didn't go to school as a full-day girl, I went half days. At home, Aleksandra Ivanovna appeared. She was a new governess. She moved into the room beside the classroom. The classroom, where so many of my teachers had lost all hope, came to life once more. It was there I spent the hours after coming home from school until bedtime; then, after washing up at my washbasin behind the folding screen, I ran in my bathrobe to my sister's bedroom and waited to say prayers with Mama. Even so, things didn't work out at school. I'd had too large a taste of freedom and made bad use of it. My pranks in class drove all my teachers wild. And when it was nearly spring, I committed a crime and was expelled: I bought a bun from Shultz and gave it to one of the boarders, the perpetually hungry Sonya Smirnova. But buns were strictly forbidden for the boarders. Sonya got caught and told on me. My action was taken for open rebellion; during dance lessons, when all the classes were gathered in the big recreation room, the principal called me up and reprimanded me, in front of the whole school. They sent a note home where they said I verbally repented of my crime. But I had no desire to repent, and, instead, was rude to Mother herself.

Mama whipped me with a birch rod and kept repeating, through tears, "Today it's not painful, just shameful. Next time it will be shameful and painful. Both shameful and painful."

I didn't forget that . . . for a long time . . .

The next day Mama went to see the principal, and after that they didn't send me to school anymore. And my life seemed to brighten up a bit.

It was interesting with Aleksandra Ivanovna. She was tall and flat and very serious—as though she knew something important and kept mournfully silent. What was it? She was serious and respectable with me, sometimes a bit sarcastic . . . but, for the time being, I put up with that, too. I got used to it. I learned a lot of German. Aleksandra Ivanovna had been born and grew up in the German provinces, although she was Russian.

The schoolroom was separated from the rest of the house by a dark room filled with cupboards, and by a dark corridor filled with cockroaches. Sounds from the other part of the family's apartment didn't come that far. The windows looked out on the courtyard. Directly opposite were the windows of the kitchen and the servants' quarters. Bobik's cage hung there; he was let out for the day to jump around and would sit on my notebook and peck at my pen. In the corner stood a screen that hid my washbasin and a cupboard, with books and jars on top for chemistry experiments. My school desk, stained with ink and the wood cut up, was covered tight with green oilcloth that crackled; there was a couchette by the wall, on which Aleksandra Ivanovna sat or lay beside a small lacquered oval table, while I did her assignments for the next morning.

Aleksandra Ivanovna had an unattractive, large face with sticking-out, colorless sad eyes without lashes. Powder for some reason snuggled in the pores of skin on her high cheeks, and dandruff in her smooth, russet hair. The dandruff fell on the oilcloth, and I always noticed it; it depressed me and made me slightly nauseated. I was unbearably fastidious.

Lessons dragged on from nine till one. During recesses I played with balls in the wardrobe room. They were a school. They came in all ages and classes. At one o'clock we had lunch, tucked in together at the very bottom of the table, and then set off for gymnastics. I walked quickly and wound up shoving Aleksandra Ivanovna inadvertently and regularly from right to left: on our way, toward the walls of buildings; coming back, toward the edge of the street. She was mildly sarcastic in reprimanding me. In general, I couldn't make out whether she respected me or held me in disdain, whether she was fond of me or indifferent.

In the evening, once I'd done my lessons, I joined her in her solitary walk from one corner of the schoolroom to the other, back and forth. I squeezed my chest up against her sharp elbow, looked up at her with ravenous eyes and asked:

"Sie lieben mich?"*

She smiled mysteriously and answered:

"Von Herzen . . ."

And then added:

"Mit Schmerzen."

* German in original. English translation: "Do you love me?" . . . "From my heart . . ." . . . "Till it hurts." . . . "A teeny bit." . . . "And not at all."—TRANS.

I cried, "Stop it."

And my heart pounded with stupid, noisy happiness. But the words kept falling evenly, with a touch of sarcasm:

"Klein wenig . . ."

I started to howl so I wouldn't hear the end. But invariably I heard it:

"Und garnicht."

And everything in the room got quiet. I didn't know if what she said was the truth or not. But my heart fell further and further. I dropped my hand and went off very quietly to wash up. Usually by then it was already time for bed.

After dinner I was allowed to play with Volodya for half an hour. But in half an hour we barely managed to hitch up the horses before the tall, flat figure of Aleksandra Ivanovna appeared in the doorway, tightly wrapped in a mohair scarf with stitches that sparkled. She called me without speaking.

While elsewhere, in distant rooms, in sitting rooms and bedrooms, the life of the grown-ups unfolded. It was the first year my sister went out. Our house belonged to Grandfather and was filled with our relatives. The servants cleaned the rooms, brought treats, and helped the frequent guests take off and put on coats in the entryway. There was laughter there, and always something happening: either performances or living pictures or an evening of dances or sledding on troikas. They sewed for the poor, and once gave lessons to the poor somewhere. Mama cried on Sundays, and the rest of the week she lived for the family, trying to be young. Sometimes my father was rarely home, sometimes always. Sometimes he was silent for days on end, other times he talked a great deal, agitatedly, endlessly recounting something disturbing, scary, and incomprehensible about some sort of important strange people with a great deal of power, whom the down-and-out don't like but who are honest and courageous . . . I didn't understand a thing and just felt surprised by something. But I loved to hear my father's animated voice, because then things grew cheerful, and sometimes my father was affectionate and looked at me fondly. When I said good-night after dinner, so as not to bother him later, he held my face to his long, soft, silky beard, and half sang the words of benediction over me, quickly making the sign of the cross above my head with his slender, beautiful hand.

There was more freedom in summer in the country. In the morning I had to get up earlier to give food and water to all my many animals, and clean their boxes. Then, of course, there were lessons with Aleksandra Ivanovna until dinner. After dinner there was croquet, and then, after milk and berries, I played with Volodya.

In the summer we were either Charlie and Lucy again, or two workers, Jack and Bob. There's lots of work. You have to plow and harrow for hours on end, patiently dragging the shovel or rake behind you down the alley, in place of a plow or harrow. You have to turn the wheel in the factory. The horse circles the tree on a rope, and the worker sits on the branch and drives him. You have to go hunting wild animals with packs of dogs. What adventures we had then! Volodya assented docilely to everything I urged on him in the whirlwind of fantasy. He was younger and more weak-willed, and had a gloomy disposition; he could be rebellious, too, but was hopeless and glum about it. Often, our games were terrible and wild, and we let out such terrible, wild yells in the grove that once, when guests were leaving the estate manager's, they returned to his office to warn him that someone was being murdered in the master's park.

But something new started this summer that, at first, quite surprised us and kept us busy.

Somehow we both understood that in this lucid, ordered, tidy life, where we seemed to tread a tightrope over water, there was something hidden from us, and what what was hidden existed not only outside us, but inside us as well. I think that's how Volodya understood it, too, not only me. Because there awoke in him an intense and burning curiosity. Once I'd understood, I took what I'd understood as another game, a new one that was alluring and bad; the soul of that game was the unknown, and what was unknown was me, and it was in my power to disclose and then again conceal that tormenting, sharply burning secret. In this new game, the evil power turned out to be mine. And when we both suddenly immersed ourselves in that life, as initiates who look endlessly for more, everything became quite different for me than it had been before. The new game now turned into torment, but we both were drawn into that torment by a power not our own.

My heart was poisoned then by great disdain for grown-ups, for people who lied to me; all intimacy vanished, and love seemed snuffed out.

Volodya became a secret accomplice instead of my comrade. Knowing our secret, we had to conceal it. That drew us terribly close, and we hated each other for that terrible, now irreparable closeness. It was as though there was a face that only we saw, no one else. It watched us, and we couldn't tear our eyes away. How were we to guess if it was for good or bad?

Entwined, perplexed, poisoned, and ill-humored—for a long time we couldn't tear away from the eyes of our secret, but suddenly we grasped that those eyes were inside us, that we were the secret. We looked inward for some answer; we were pathetic, we were filled with hate: Volodya from ravenous impotence, and I from evil triumph.

Toward spring, one Sunday night, we started a new game at Grandfather's.

A General Popov moved in under Grandfather's apartment, replacing one of the aunts, who for some reason had moved. When we

ran like wild horses or galloped the circus tightrope down the hall
by the Devil's closet, General Popov would send his butler with the
humble request that we not pound our feet above his head.

Once we'd pounded out our energy and ill temper at his request,
Volodya and I slipped out that evening to the front stairway, ran up
to our floor, and rang the bell. The dishwasher opened the door;
she'd been left alone to keep an eye on the house and went off to her
place in the kitchen, far away . . .

In Volodya's nursery it was quiet and strange. The clock ticked,
there was a rustling in the corners and behind the walls, our voices
sounded empty and echoing, and my heart beat in my chest . . .

We built our train and hitched up the horses. We laughed loudly and to no purpose, pretended to quarrel, then grew suddenly
silent, listening to the emptiness, the quiet, the rustle of walls and
corners, the thudding of our hearts . . .

We abandoned the unhitched chairs, wandered from room to
hall, and burst ahead with wide-open eyes and flared-out nostrils,
whining quietly from a sudden, wild, stuffy fear, through the entry
hall to the stairway and down the stairs, always with the same low
whine: after all, the wall from the entry hall was glass and it was visible to *them*—everything was visible . . . They see *us*, we just don't
see *them* . . .

Grandfather's.

In the enfilade sitting room behind the trellis.

Here, in the illuminated boredom between the two rooms, where
the aunts, uncles, and cousins are, it was better, much better. We
caught our breath on the small sofa, and then set to playing school.

Lessons. Andrew, Lucy, Charlie, all having classes.

"Volodya, did you see that on the glass?"

"Who?"

"I don't know. When we were running out."

"What?"

"Pressed against the glass . . ."

"That's stupid. Do you know how much one thousand and one thousand is?"

"Two thousand, Mister Charlie."

"That's not right."

And suddenly Mister Charlie's rosy cheeks grow pale with anger.

"That's not right. You haven't learned your lesson, Lucy. I'll have to punish you! To the Devil's closet with you. You'll get a whipping . . ."

I don't cry. All the boys are surprised that I don't cry. I look with crazed audacity at Mister Charlie's pale face. Mister Charlie's nostrils quiver and his blue eyes flash, just as they do when I tease him and he throws himself at me with a knife, a stick, a rock, suddenly strong and frightening. But I'm not frightened now. And I whisper quietly:

"You're not going to whip me."

Of course the boys are watching, they're surprised, they're waiting . . . There are lots of them. I'm alone. I have to live up to the name of Princess . . . But Mister Charlie calls Bob and Jack. They lead me off.

I go. I see there's no point in struggling. Or in calling out. We go out that way beyond the trellis; we run into one aunt and two cousins.

"What a mean face you have, little Vera!"

As well I might! They don't see Jack and Bob. They don't know that Volodya is Mister Charlie and that they're taking me to be whipped.

It's dark and stuffy in the Devil's closet. They throw me on the floor. They take my clothes off to whip me. It's all the same to me; I'm self-assured and undefeatable. They beat the martyrs that way, but they couldn't dishonor them. Volodya beats me with his little hand. Of course it hurts something awful. I don't cry out . . .

And suddenly I'm defeated. I'm defeated in myself. That's how I want it. The blows, the stuffy darkness, the secrecy, all are sweet to me, together with the burning shame of the Devil's closet.

From that time on, every game became that one. Every game, so we could say to each other: let's go play this or that. But our eyes understood and tried not to meet each other.

In the country there was a tent. A real tent: white with a red border. A stake had been driven in the meadow, and the tent was stretched on pegs into a broad circle. We played factory. Volodya sat on a larch branch and beat me with a long whip. The rope turned round the tree and my head spun so that I fell to the ground with a wheezing moan. Then he kicked his horse till she got up, and he drove her into the tent.

The horse took sick. From the sun and the circling the horse got dizzy. She'll have to be treated. A veterinarian treats her in the tent. Volodya is the vet . . .

"Vera, why aren't you acting right?"

"I am."

"Not really."

"I can. I just don't want to right now."

Volodya grovels . . . I lie there and listen to a bee as it buzzes and thuds against the tent fabric, as my heart thuds in my chest, and it buzzes in my head. You come out of the milky half-light, where it smells of grass and roots, the sun blinds you, and your cheeks are drenched with warmth.

"Volodya, why are people ashamed of each other? We won't be."

"We never will be."

In our country house there's a large room, two different shades of paint, cut off from the dining room by a narrow, dark parlor. To the right and left it's like two burrows, almost all filled up with two massive, ancient, oilcloth sofas. Volodya and I crawled down the broad, cool oilcloth to the very darkest place. I'm first. He's behind.

If you look into the darkness for a long time, with your nose stuck up against the oilcloth, you'll see a bright little devil: a small one, that glows like a wolf's eye at night . . .

Beyond the grove there's a stream overgrown with thick bushes. We would take our clothes off. Nobody knew. We went swimming. We looked at each other. I wanted to do something worse. Worse. I thought things up that would be even worse and was surprised when it didn't turn out the way I wanted, the way it was, the way it should have been. And if it could have been worse still, completely shameful, that would have been fine.

We lived on with our secret, where I was strong in willful weakness and in the power of refusal; where Volodya burned in impotence and spite. We lived among grown-ups we deceived and who deceived us, and we found it amusing and disgusting, and we were proud. And I loved to embarrass the grown-ups with words, once I realized what words would embarrass them.

In the winter we were reading something . . . about some people or other and their beliefs. I asked Aleksandra Ivanovna:

"Everyone believes in their own God. Why is ours the real one?"

"I promised your mama not to talk with you about religion. Go ask her."

Then I understood her secret, and that there was no God.

II. The Whip

There was something I longed for.

What I longed for was a whip. A whip that I could stick into the front of the cart.

My desire was born once I'd broken in Ruslan and rode on him to visit the village medic I was in love with.

Breaking in Ruslan was hard: it was quite an achievement. One-on-one, an unequal battle, since the time I crawled out from under the overturned cart and looked up achingly from my ditch toward the abandoned road, peeved at the stubborn donkey. Meanwhile, once he'd torn the harness straps, he nibbled and chewed the juicy grass with good-hearted compusure.

To come up from behind and hit him in the shafts was unpleasant: Ruslan would happily kick up both back hooves. From the muzzle, holding him by the reins, was pointless. Ruslan showed his teeth and bared his whole red gum with its yellow, still young teeth; he didn't even turn his head, and he stared at me angrily with his violet-white eyes.

That's when the battle would begin.

I clasped his gentle gray neck, tensed my narrow chest and muscular stomach, and rammed the enemy with rapid, shoving smacks up the bank till he moved his stubborn legs from the dank bottom earth where he'd planted them.

He stamped in place and kneaded the muck in the ditch with his inconvenienced hooves; then at last Ruslan made up his mind, headed slowly away from me, and clambered onto the road.

With two jumps I was ahead of him, grabbed his coarse-haired withers, jumped onto his sharp backbone, clenched my legs on the splayed sides of his grayish paunch, gave the reins a tug, whooped, and took off at a jolting, deftly short-paced gallop; we left the overturned cart with its four wheels up in the air and headed down the familiar, inescapable road that led to the stables.

But by the time my desire was born, the heroic time of battle was already far behind, and it seemed impossible to repeat the past. Now Ruslan took me at a trot and a gallop down forest, field, and country roads. I took the priest's daughter riding and the daughter of the estate manager, once even Aleksandra Ivanovna, my governess, who hated ditches, and once—even her, the village medic herself.

But Volodya I didn't take riding. Volodya said it was boring on a donkey. But he was just scared, because he was such a coward.

That's when it was, when I took the village medic riding, that the desire was born.

The desire for a whip.

A whip to stick into the front of the cart. A whip with a tall curved stem, an elegant narrow twist, and a long, narrow, tightly woven strap.

I could feel it in my hand; I sensed the pliant slaps of the cane stem on my clenched fingers; I saw its slender high line arched before me and the twist, from which, of course, there would never be a sharp stick jutting out, as there was on my small play whips.

And from that happy morning, when I took my first love riding through fragrant spring greenery, this newly born desire quite befuddled me.

I waved my clenched-fisted empty hand decisively forward with a sharp crack, then jerked back my forearm deftly. Then I heard the dry, sharp slap of the whip I so longed for, with its silky tassel on the end of a narrow strap; the long, finely turned strap cut the air with a whip and a whistle. And even when I closed my eyes with pleasure and bitter fear, I saw how the donkey, once stung by the sound, twitched his ears, waved his tail, and moved his gray mass forward, and I fell back, buckled at the waist, as if at the sudden jolting of my cart.

I started to live for my desire.

I brought my desire from the country into town. It entwined my mind and heart like a spider's web—soft, slender, but tenacious.

My desire gave me life.

It was so beautiful. It called to me with pressure quite supple. It seemed unattainable and inescapable. And no matter what I did, what I thought or said, my hand closed on the delicate cane, the line of the light, elegant twist struck my eyes and with a shudder I listened for the sharp slap of the whip, dry as a shot.

And my desire was enflamed by the impossibility of fulfillment. Who among *them* could understand how imperative it was. *They* didn't understand either Ruslan or the whip or me. And they laughed because their life was boring and pale.

But I was the poorer one, because I didn't have enough to pay for the fulfillment of my wishes. All I had was fifty-three kopeks. While a whip . . . what could such a wonderful whip cost?

Maybe fifty-five roubles?

All the same, I had to have what I wanted. All the same, that was how it turned out, that I wanted to possess the whip.

How strange it became, living in this year of the whip, without God.

For there was no God. But God commands us to be honest and obedient, to honor our parents and teachers. To study and overcome our desires.

He doesn't exist. But desire does.

And not only one. If you have one big one, then other ones, smaller, will follow. Many, many smaller ones.

The small desires are all sharp and rough. Like a bunch of horsehair sticking through a mattress. They prickle. Lots of small, rough, prickly desires.

And God does not exist.

It's convenient. Much more convenient.

Of course I didn't go to Mama. How could I tell Mama that there is no God? Because then nothing exists. Nothing that's real exists. And it's all just pretend, not for real, so let's be quick about it and as merry as we can, so we'll forget . . .

But when Mama looks at me, with her big, sad eyes, I know that everything is real and important and forever.

It's frightening and inconvenient.

And it's frightening without it, because . . . horror of horrors, sin to end all sin, suddenly to believe that there is no God! I'd never have dared say words like that to anyone! And I didn't tell Volodya. I just knew it—those words, and all of life, all people, all things became alien to me.

And I looked at everyone and everything with new, startled eyes, with rapid, greedy glances, and in everything and everyone saw only my own desires.

But in all my desires I saw only that one desire.

And that desire was somehow tied to this new world of mine, in which there was such unexpected space, such emptiness and lightness, because it was a world without God.

Of course no one but me knew this last secret. Only I knew, and I was silent.

Or did everyone know and keep silent? The way everyone, of course, knew that other secret, the shameful one, and kept silent . . .

I organized an auction.

I brought all sorts of old toys and things to the sitting room, where they allowed me to stay after dinner.

There was a curved tin nightingale on a whistle, which I used to improve the singing of my lame canary, Bobik. There was a frame with a little glass where there once had been a picture of mountains, now worn off. And a little whatnot that I had poorly cut and lazily glued together, and a shabby enameled paper knife with a picture of the dawn and a pretty girl by a gate. Those I remember. And there were lots of things besides, broken, shabby things I didn't want anymore.

I needed money to buy a whip, so I put the auction together. I jacked up the prices, knocked with my hammer, held my brothers to their word, saying that anyone who repeated the whole price as they raised a bid had to pay twice . . .

I could tell that Mama was out of sorts, that my sister was fright-

ened by my greed, that it was repulsive in the room. My loud voice
and agitated laughter, my clapping hands are crushing the salty,
slippery worm, but still it creeps from my chest alive, up into my
throat, from my throat into my mouth, into my nose, and I want to cry.

Behind the screen in the schoolroom, where my washstand is
concealed, I spread out my loot beside the soap dish: three roubles,
twenty-two kopeks.

And fifty-three kopeks more in my purse. Altogether, three roubles, seventy-five kopeks. Enough to buy a whip?

At lunch I'll ask my middle brother, my kind, cheerful brother;
he knows everything and wasn't at the auction.

But maybe he's home already now? I'll run to his room.

I tear along. As I go I'm already calling out, "Kolya! Kolya-a-a!
Kolya-a-a!"

I burst through the door.

Empty.

I want to leave. I've already turned back. But I've seen something, with my overly farsighted eyes. (They're even thinking of
treating this unhealthy farsightedness.) And that means what I'd
seen didn't reach my soul, but stayed in my eyes alone. I'm urged
on, by something, toward something, heavy and drowsy, toward
the window where a large desk stands. And already I seem caught
unaware, and my heart pulls back.

Already I'm at the desk. A pile of coins is scattered on blue cloth.

The coins belong to Kolya, to my cheerful, affectionate Kolya.

I'll ask him . . .

My hand stretched out . . .

And a sudden sharp joy, malicious but very calm and clear, filled
my chest and head. My heart even jumped, but quietly, so even it
wouldn't hear, and mocking, gay thoughts got inaudibly entangled
in their own lackluster web.

Now there are four roubles, twelve kopeks, on the washstand.

Just so long as no one steals them! I hide them in a money box and throw the money box under the bureau. Tanya doesn't ever sweep under there . . .

I'll wait for Kolya. He'll take me on his trotter to the store; we'll buy the whip together! I'll hang it up till spring . . . (Oh, how long it is till spring! But no matter, I need the whip as soon as possible, I can't wait any longer! . . .) I'll hang it on the wall above the school desk. It will be fun to do my lessons and snap it . . . I mean, of course, she won't let me snap it, but I'll imagine doing it.

Kolya is so wonderful, he'll go.

What a time it is! It seems that nothing's impossible: all you have to do is want it!

There's buried treasure everywhere.

On the windowsill in Mother's room, under the hatbox, there's a large box full of gingerbread made with honey. I emptied it slowly, patiently, fearlessly, day by day, to the bottom. Nobody found out.

The day began with the honey gingerbread, and then dragged on further, minute by minute, minute by separate minute, separate and forgettable. And each one, once over, died forgotten, while the next one, full of hunger, looked into my empty, unsated eyes, cold and fearlessly gleaming. We blinked at each other in recognition: an hour till death, what's done—I'll forget. That is freedom.

I lied. Because lying kills. It became quite convenient, because without God I grew more cunning. The desires had taught me that. I almost never got caught, and my empty eyes always burned with cold delight. Eyes impenetrable beyond their brilliance.

I loved the lie.

Everything that led from one thing to another, one thing recalling the other, loving the other, dying for the other, purifying it, pledging its life for what had died, leading on despite impediment, bearing tirelessly the sacred thread forged of links from Beginning to Beginning, fearsome, holy, immutable Necessity—the lie cut short, and established Empty Freedom.

They punished me less. No doubt because I had more frequent recourse to lying, and when I didn't it was all the same to me. Whether in the corner or confined to the schoolroom, thoughts came to me that were amusing, uninhibited, and without shame.

The games with Volodya had almost stopped of their own accord; they all led to that one same game. When our eyes met they gleamed with torment, and I taught him how to deceive.

That was inside. I don't remember any major events or external acts of daring. Just that my gaze turned from inward out.

At moments I was seized by horror.

For Volodya I had no mercy. The blame for the dirty notebook I shifted to him. Horse heads on the penmanship lessons, horned ones, very badly drawn in blood. The idea had been mine, as was the realization.

I didn't even tell Volodya. He was still stupid, afraid of blood, and therefore contemptible.

This was how it happened. I suddenly got bored as I was drawing the beautiful letters, so bored that all hope vanished of eluding that even, gray boredom, flat and mute. And through the gray muteness, as through a mute gray sky, slashed gleams of summer lightning . . .

It was them—my desires. Though they, too, were totally hopeless, because I only wanted what didn't exist. It came clear in all the murk, clear to the point of tears, that I wanted nothing that existed, only that which was nowhere to be found.

Then I took the knife and started cutting my hand above the wrist, where the blue veins are right beneath the skin. I scratched and the pain was burning, I wheezed in a kind of disgusting way, was scared by my own wheezing, and threw the knife away. The trickle of blood flowed slowly, drop by narrow drop pressing out of the wound.

Then I wanted to dirty the penmanship notebook, and, once I'd dipped a pen into a drop, I drew a horse.

I was drawing a horse, beginning from the head, and it didn't come out right, so I had to start again, but the blood was clotting and I had to suck at it and moisten the salty metal nib. That's how the awkward bloody horse heads all came out with ears that looked like horns.

And *she* asked:

"Who smeared red devils here?"

It amused me and cheered me up, and, without thinking why, without any ulterior motives in mind, I answered:

"Volodya."

And I whimpered, holding back tears.

She still doubted me. She came right up and looked in my teary eyes.

"Can you give me your word it was him and not you?"

"Word of honor."

"And what sort of disgusting paint is this, just like blood?"

I rattled off words of honor at one go, then lifted my proud head with its shining, empty eyes, impudent and greedy.

I'll never forget the way my eyes were then. I would stare into the mirror sometimes as I brushed my thin, tangled, ash-blond hair. I was beautiful then from the luster of my eyes in fair hair.

Why not give one's word of honor, if you can lie? It's all the same. I always liked to take everything to extremes.

And why not betray Volodya, if everything's completely apart, and you need to be happy?

Why not?

He can do it, too, if he wants. I won't be offended.

Once Aleksandra Ivanovna and I were in a shop buying notebooks for me. There were splinter wood boxes with something in them, and I desperately wanted to know what. I moved my muff along the table, snatched back my hand. When we came out onto the street I felt, with my slightly trembling fingers: two splinter boxes.

At home I divided up the loot this way: one box for myself, the other for Aleksandra Ivanovna, to taunt her, and because it was pleasant. She looked at me so hard it was dreadful, but she took it.

There were Chinese flowers in the boxes. If you put them into water, they start to bloom.

Tanya had been dismissed. Kolya had noticed at that point that the coins were missing from his desk, and had told. They waited a bit. And then it was the gingerbread. Sugar from the pantry, and . . . then more and more ten-kopeck coins from table. In the purse above my bureau there was five and a half roubles in all.

I saved Kolya for the last.

We press close together in the narrow sled. He's clasped me by the waist. A broad cloth cuts off the light right ahead, in front of our noses. If you thrust your head to one side to look, biting cold snow from under the horseshoes hits you in the eyes. The wind grabbed skin and stretched it too taut across faces.

Painful and exhilarating.

Then, the smell of finished leather, the gleam of polished copper, bridles, harness, saddles, saddles, saddles!

This is heaven!

I'm excited, extremely excited. So much so it seems that I can't see a thing.

And suddenly the whip!

It's in front of me. Kolya holds it in his hands. And I must be afraid. How dreadful it is when suddenly the thing you lived for comes about.

What I had longed for I had lived for.

And what next? . . .

It was made of cane. I rubbed with my finger down the shiny lacquered stem, with small knobs where branches had been lopped off.

Kolya placed it in my hand. It was light; the cane stem thrust upward and the lithe, tightly wound, narrow strap twisted elegantly at the top. Then and there I slapped the silken tassel against my cheek.

I walked off to one side, where there was room.

Gripping the supple handle, I waved my empty hand decisively forward with a sharp crack, then jerked back my forearm deftly. Then I heard how the newly acquired whip slapped dry and sharp with its silken tassel on the end of the narrow strap, how the long, elegantly wound strap cut the air with a whip and whistle.

We went up . . . I handed the whip over to someone. It was quiet and confused inside me.

As we rode home, I clutched the whip in its wrapping of thin paper adoringly in my hand. My quiet dissolved in the rushing air and keen frost, and suddenly I was full of chatter and plans.

"Kolya, you know what I think? We could harness Lyudmila to Ruslan as a trace horse."

Lyudmila was his wife, with a darker coat, a narrow head, and a sharp, humped back. She stumbled along helplessly on aching legs. Every spring she gave birth to a stillborn foal.

Kolya objected:

"She wears pasterns. She doesn't bend her legs at the hooves. You can't."

"That doesn't matter. It doesn't matter at all!" I spoke hastily, already tingling with longing. "You know what? It doesn't hurt her. Sometimes she comes running along with us all by herself."

"With whom?"

"With me and Ruslan."

"And who are you?"

I wasn't listening. It's always the same with my brothers. Sometimes I got mad, sometimes I fought. Today there was no time to be offended.

"See, if you have a whip, then it works well as a team. But I like to have a trace horse. I'll harness Lyudmila with ropes. I can do it myself. I don't want leather traces."

"But how can you do that—an English whip, but with peasant ropes, like a cart?"

"It doesn't matter, really, it doesn't matter. In fact, you know, that's what's good. A whip and ropes. I don't like it when it's the way it should be. The whip—is in your hand."

And I'm clutching it, clutching it. I didn't yet believe it—and grew just a bit sad, from contempt, just the slightest contempt for it: for now it was mine, and I no longer pined for it, no longer pined for it, with hot raptures, scorching blood, my life.

"But with a pair of donkeys—they'll run along smart! Lyudmila will go at a gallop. Kolya, you know what? I'll harness her head from the side and she'll gallop. Kolya, will we keep up with you? What do you think?"

"So you'll go at a gallop, too?"

He's still making fun of me. But you can't get angry with him, and it's much too interesting . . .

"You'll go after black grouse, and we'll go, too."

"They only shoot the brood in autumn."

"And what about spring? Kolya? What's in the spring?"

"In the spring? Snipe. Mating."

"Then I'll go everywhere with you. You can shoot snipe with a Montecristo."

"Are you going to shoot?"

"Why not?"

"But you're always praying for rabbits. Remember how Antip caught you on your knees?"

That's Antip, the forester. I was ashamed to remember it: my brothers took me rabbit hunting, and I said prayers.

"What rubbish! I'm not at all that way now. I'm going to shoot."

We were already running up our staircase. We rang at the entryway.

While we waited for them to open the door, I threw my arms round him and thanked him, overcome once more by undiluted delight.

I ran down the corridor without having taken off my fur coat and galoshes, turned into the wardrobe room, in the middle of which stood a portable stepladder (Volodya and I made a circus on it), went up the winding stairs to the platform, jumped from the heights, holding the whip above my head in both hands, and then again . . . Back to the spiral and the bug-sized steps. Hop, hop. And I burst in the door of the schoolroom.

She's not sitting on her couchette. Maybe she's in her room?

Her room is right next door.

Yes. She's reading in her armchair by the table.

"Aleksandra Ivanovna! A whip, a whip, a whip!"

She seemed a bit frightened. I had probably been very impetuous and emphatic when I said it. And she couldn't get used to it. And then I was in my fur coat and galoshes . . .

I rip off the thin, silky paper. I jump off to one side where there's room. With a sharp crack I strike my hand forward, the handle clutched passionately in my trembling fingers, and pull back my forearm with a sudden agile jerk. I heard how the whip, now mine, snapped dry and sharp with its silky tassel at the end of the narrow strap, and the elegantly turned strap cut the air with a whip and a whistle, and the bliss of possession and pride lashed sharp at my heart.

With the affrontery of abundance, I stood and looked at her there in the armchair, skinny and hapless; I looked into her temperate eyes, pale from a bloodless life, shortsighted, protuberant, luster-less—and into her flat, broad-cheeked face, with muscles that had dried out and hardened like wood, stretching the corners of her long mouth somewhat downward.

And I kick up my heels in front of her, in my fur coat and ga-loshes, my hair disheveled, since I'd torn off my hat while still in the entryway. I'm already teasing in advance, sensing that my joy will be rebuffed, will be extinguished.

"What is all this?" She asked quite pointlessly in her hollow voice. She could very well see and hear.

By way of response, I slapped with the whip once more, no longer stepping to one side with it, right there beside her, and she drew back, her broad, flat chest shuddering abruptly in the mohair dress.

"You've gone mad. Or are you being impudent? And what do you need that whip for?"

"For Ruslan and Lyudmila."

"How much did you pay for it?"

"Kolya bought it."

"Then how much did he pay?"

I thought about it. There, at the cashier's, Kolya took the money I'd collected and hidden, but then he added his own. I had seen how he took from his purse a blue, five-rouble note, just like mine, and paid with both of them, then gave me back my rouble and all the change and said: "We'll split the cost. I'll pay half."

Kolya, Kolya. There's no brother more dear! It's good he wasn't at that embarrassing auction.

"Ten roubles," I figured.

Aleksandra Ivanovna straightened in her armchair; the even pallor of her eyes glimmered suddenly with a luster different than that sparked in her by fastidious offense at my usual crude stubborness and "acting up" . . .

Just before she spoke—she didn't speak at once—I understood

from the gleam that blazed up in her eyes that this was anger, and that anger such as this was righteous.

And I rebelled.

I rebelled because, for the first time, I perceived anger as righteous anger. I rebelled against what was righteous, for when Righteousness summons, there are two paths: the path of submission and hosannas or the path of rebellion and damnation.

And it was strange to me that righteousness suddenly appeared in her, precisely in her—someone who had never, ever, understood anything real.

Now she was speaking. And her voice was not the normal, dreary one—instead, it rang like the voice that speaks words of righteousness.

"You are a good-for-nothing girl who has never given a thought to others. Do you realize that there are children who have nothing to eat, that not only are they unable to buy whips and ride on donkeys, but their souls and minds remain in darkness and throughout their whole bodies there is but one thought: what is there to eat, because their stomachs are pinched and aching constantly? Did you think . . . did you think that with these ten roubles a girl like you can be fed for a month, her mind could have the nourishment of learning, which you have in such abundance that you revolt against and torment those to whom you should be thankful?"

Aleksandra Ivanovna said much more, all in the same agitated, vibrant voice, all the same righteous and indubitable words, but I no longer heard them all, because the more indubitable and righteous they became, the more spitefully furious was my hopeless rebellion; I kicked up my heels and whistled and grimaced grotesquely, and met those vibrant, righteous words with the sharp, piercing steel of my heart, so that they flew at me dead already and incapable of speech.

"You cry about canaries and dogs, but when children right beside you are dying, children like you who have never known what happiness is—it's none of your business, you don't even notice . . . If you knew, experienced it, even just once experienced it . . . if rich people like you could feel it in your heart, and raised your children differently . . . . if *you*, heartless girl . . . damn your whip, your damned whip! You, Miss Grimace Face, you clown, are simply an idiot."

My heart seemed to have been waiting for that; it stretched out farther and farther from my breast, a sharp sword, one brilliant strip of steel, stretching toward this vicious, true word. My coarse mouth screamed:

"You're an idiot yourself."

That was the blow of my steel.

She stood and put her hard, severe hand on my shaking shoulder and led me toward the door.

"Get out."

"I will not."

"You are going out."

"Don't you dare push me."

She pushes me. She pushes without even knowing that she's pushing, because her blood, which had always been restrained and reined in by life, flared up and burned with righteous anger.

We grabbed at each other.

It was horrible.

Rebellion and Anger did battle, and Rebellion tore the black mohair shawl that lay on Anger's breast. Anger tore at Rebellion's hair and pushed her out the door, and for a long time Rebellion beat Anger's door with clenched fists, crying with the thin whining howl . . . of a dog.

III. The Small Red Spider

Our guiding illusions.

I heard those words later, when I was already grown, from one of my friends, when I confessed to her what the purple-blazed wings of dawn had promised.

Our guiding illusions! In everyone they appear and beckon onward, she said, beckon onward, leading on and on along paths of torment and paths of bliss, of sin and pleasure, partings and expectations—toward truth.

That spring, when I learned of my expulsion, my guiding illusions were—mattresses . . ..

This is how it happened.

A council of family and doctors was called. There was Aunt Klavdia and Uncle Andriusha (the one who loved Mama and didn't love me because I tormented her), my two older brothers, my sister, *her,* Mama herself, our regular home doctor and a second doctor he'd asked to come, and a famous psychiatrist.

First of all, the doctors undressed me and spent a long time poking at my chest, my stomach, my back, my knees. I was in a bad mood and felt ashamed but was overcome by the unexpectedness and ceremony of it all.

Then Mama started talking in a strange voice, frightened and stumbling, and she talked for a long time about how not one governess had been able to teach me and that Aleksandra Ivanovna, too, had given up all hope.

Then Aleksandra Ivanovna spoke in a monotone, flat and without pausing, and gave an account of the whip and the fight; then Uncle spoke, but by then I wasn't listening; I tore from my seat and ran out of the room, frowning so hard that my bad-temper wrinkle dug deep across my forehead above my nose.

Of course, they had noticed that when that wrinkle digs in there's no stopping me, so they didn't pursue me.

I sat, of course, in the wardrobe, under my sister's ball gowns. The only difference between this and the times before was that I wasn't crying.

Something had been affronted, something had been forever affronted, and that feeling of forever was new and forced me for the first time to feel myself a wholly real person.

Toward night, when they'd exhausted themselves with running around looking for me, I crawled out and crept into my bed, where they found me asleep. Of course, I was only pretending. Even for Mama I didn't open my eyes, even when she blessed me—I felt nothing. Like a log.

Lessons with Aleksandra Ivanovna continued. The day crawled along as before, but everything was new, not real. Because life couldn't be as before, and real, if they hadn't punished me after the whip.

I was quite sick at heart, terribly, absolutely alone. It was because they hadn't punished me. It was so wildly improbable, so unjust, that the "unrealness" of life was more probable.

Of course, all this only seems to be just for a minute, a day, maybe two, and it will turn out she's not real and I'm not real, nor is Mama, and the classroom's not real and nothing exists.

Simple and absolute: nothing exists.

She was always writing something. Mama for some reason came in to see us often, something she'd never done before . . . Why would *she* be writing? Big dictionaries were brought in. Why does Mama need to smile at me, to smile so shyly, as she walks through the classroom to her own room?

They left the classroom when Prokofy announced supper. They called me, both of them affectionate . . . I didn't go right away. I said I would wash my hands behind the screen. Alone, I went in to *her* room.

A large sheet of notepaper forgotten on her table. I made for the paper: in German.

I look. The lines start to dance. Why? What do I fear? The answer to the riddle. Now, right now, I will find out why this whole life isn't real, and what sort of life it really is. And I don't want to.

I'm not up to it.

I want to tear myself from the crossed-out, scribbled-in lines of the German draft, and I can't. Some inner will impels me, holds me above the paper.

I need to. Need to.

This ponderous will presses on toward the riddle's answer . . . freely, it goes to meet it, not to accept it but to claim it.

"Die Gesellschaft von Madchen ihres Alters unter Eurer frommen Obhut . . . Das bessere Clima Eurer Heimath . . . Eure Gute, hochgeehrte Schwester . . . Die Religionsfrage . . . Es Giebt ja nur Einen Gott fur Alle."*

So . . . some of it I understand. But I could understand still less and still understand it all.

I stood there, astonished. Stood . . . Stood . . .

Then I walked from the room through the classroom, through the corridor and wardrobe room, another corridor, into the dining room . . .

I saw one of the wardrobes open, a dead mouse's tail sticking out from under the bureau across from Mama's door, the mouse's back end gnawed away—no doubt it was the cat. I saw a grimace through

---

* German in the original. "The society of girls of her age in your pious keeping . . . The better climate of your homeland . . . Your goodness, highly honored Sister . . . The religious question . . . There is just one God for all. . . ."— TRANS.

the glass wall in the entry that led onto the stairway. The grimace pressed up against the glass. We often saw it Sunday evenings when Volodya and I played alone in the empty apartment. In the pantry I saw Prokofy's mocking red face.

"You're late, missy, they'll punish you and not give you dessert."

In the dining room, of course, no one punished me, no one was waiting, no one noticed. So that's how it is now . . .

I ate, chewing on something anyway, not thinking about anything. Lunch ended.

"Today we won't go to gymnastics. You can play ball in the storeroom."

I should have been happy. A weekday holiday! Instead of the hateful gymnastics in some indifferent hall, where you throw out your legs and hands on command, ahead, to the side, and up, marching stupidly without the cleverness of a game—the dodging game—in the School for Balls.

But that's how it would be—a holiday—if this were real life, but now, when everything is pretend, what joy is there in it?

I'm glad I saw a crack in the wardrobe as I went through the wardrobe room. I remembered it now on my way back.

And I'm there, beneath the silky skirts.

My dear schoolroom! My beloved Aleksandra Ivanovna!

"Mommy, my mommy, my maisy, my daisy, my deary, dear daisy, my maisy, my dear . . ."

It came out in rhyme, and I stopped my weeping and wailing.

Why are they driving me out?

Where are they driving me to?

Who will give orders now?

Will they always give orders?

Are they completely indifferent to me now?

And voiceless rebellion seized hold of me.

From the wardrobe I went to the window in Mama's empty

room. I opened the high venting window, jumped onto the windowsill, then higher onto the box of honey gingerbread I'd emptied; up to my waist, I thrust out into frosty air, gasping it with greedy, passionate sorrow into a chest inflamed with tearless sobbing.

And I longed to die.

To die, so they would forgive, and so they would repent . . .

And so everything would be over.

When I'd grown thoroughly chilled I crawled down, and since I'd gotten frozen and thought I would die soon, my heart softened and I started to cry, bitterly and abundantly, curled up like a snake at the foot of Mama's bed.

That's how Mama found me. She rushed to close the window, scolded me, sat down beside me, and took my hands from my swollen face, stroked me gently, and asked:

"What is this about? What?"

"I don't want to go to a German school."

She forgot to be surprised that I knew. She herself started to cry and, through her tears, said much that was true:

"Before God, I am doing my duty, my little one!"

And she explained to me how I was guilty and how I could be saved.

Ruslan and Lyudmila must have flashed through my mind in those hurried moments, along with the turtles, the pond with the raft that sank down to my ankles when I pushed off, Volodya, Bob, Jack, Andrew, and Mister Charlie and Lucy, and simply Charlie, and the tent with the milky light and the bumblebee, and once more the schoolroom, for one last time dear to me, and the ticklish mohair shawl. And . . . how Mama smells of mignonette! Like that shoe of Nadya's, my brother's fiancée, that I stole and took to bed to kiss and love last spring, when she was still his fiancée . . .

And suddenly Shultz, suddenly Shultz, or rather the rose-colored comb and the forget-me-not bouquet on the blotting paper. And the pool of tears beneath Gurkovich's nose, mottled Gurkovich, nose down on the table . . .

More German girls! Again it will be a German school, only this time a real one.

"Mama, why do I have to go to a German school? Why do I have to go to a foreign school? I don't like Germans."

I was so unhappy in the German school here, as a half-day girl, even when I still slept at home, but now I'd sleep in Germany, and sleep alone in Germany.

Wavelets! White, smooth sand, and wavelets have cut sharp little rows, like snakes intertwined. My bare feet remember it . . . And the dew, early, at dawn in the meadow to the sea, the pale rose carnations . . . The old barge bottom up, holes in it. Volodya and I on the upside-down bottom, our legs stuck through the holes, we row with long poles like oars, digging at sand like water . . .

"Mama, is it forbidden to go barefoot there?"

"Barefoot?"

Mama livens up, wipes her tears with a handkerchief.

And suddenly—mattresses!

Mama told me about the mattresses.

What power in these mattresses, fantastically imagined, never to be realized; they turned all the tenacious, clinging anguish of parting into greedy gladness, brilliant longing. Where had Mama heard about them? Why did it occur to her to tell me about them? And she continued:

In the German school the girls do everything for themselves; they have monitor duty two weeks at a time either in the sleeping halls or the dining room or the corridor, but each Saturday, everyone in the school hauls their mattresses out to a small meadow (they must throw them out the windows) and beats them with cane rods.

Two times a week they take clothes to the poor . . . The sisters are kind; the school was founded by an order of Protestant deaconess sisters . . .

I wasn't listening. I saw a small green meadow, rows of girls, rows of mattresses, rows of flapping cane, the intermittent flat noise, the sunshine.

Everything new, everything fantastic and independent, because I so loved to do everything myself. That was independence.

The schoolroom grew hateful again, irrevocably so, and the old life lost its color. My wanderer heart rushed forward, toward the new, the unexperienced, the suddenly enticing.

It was betrayal, and I was the traitor. Through all the folly of my happiness I observed myself and was surprised at myself, and didn't understand. Mama was quite offended and could no longer hold me with tenderness.

But I had no need of it. Greed held me. It held me tenderly, with promise and desires.

Our guiding illusions!

The mattresses proved illusory.

At the deaconesses' school (when Mama wasn't around, my playful older sister called them deaconettes) the girls didn't beat their mattresses on a meadow. At the school it was boring, tedious, and gloomy.

Through the wide corridors that cut in half the dark brick three-story building with bars on the lower windows, the deaconess sisters slipped purposefully along, their footfalls silent, in dark blue dresses and white caps with starched ruffles; they smiled pallidly, tirelessly vigilant of quiet and decorum. Two pastors directed our studies: Herr Pastor Steffan, fair-haired and short-legged, with a belly that quivered; and Herr Pastor Hattendorf, a handsome young man but crippled, with chestnut curls and dark blue eyes.

My older friends fell in love with him, cried over him, fought over him.

But not Lucia, of course, not Lucia. She was mine . . .

I watched through the window as the handsome young man stepped through the gate in the tall dark brick wall; he went down the sandy yard to the porch, limping slightly on one foot—and his crooked stick legs disgusted me, hung as they were with rumpled cloth, diligently reminiscent of prior usage. And I couldn't understand why the coarse, beastlike hair that covered his delicate cheeks and chin was so highly esteemed.

At the bright window beside me I saw Lucia's pale face, with lilac rings around gray doomed eyes. The light waves of her two dark chestnut braids flowed out like copper.

Lucia had consumption. She had been born in Alexandria, in Egypt. At first her mother educated her in Smyrna, in the same kind of deaconesses' school as here on the Rhine. Then she moved her here, to the North. Her mother must not have loved Lucia. But Lucia was afraid to admit it. And she was dying in silence.

Lucia was older than me. She was one of the "big" girls, but she "went with" me, and I was deeply proud of it.

I was in love with Lucia.

When all of a sudden she threw her two thin, slight, dryly burning arms round my neck, sorrowful, tender, and frightened, then drew back and looked into my eyes, rays of lilac burning in her tear-filled eyes—the minutes blurred, and time, like a heart that skips a beat, stopped on one pulse.

It was terrifying. Like a sharp descent down an icy slope. Like the threat of death.

Lucia was fateful. No doubt because she was fated to die soon. It lay in her, her impending death, although none of us, not even Lucia herself, knew it.

I met with Lucia in the garden, in corridors, and on walks, when we didn't have to walk in pairs and they let us mingle—because we were in different classes and different families.

Our girls were divided by the deaconesses into "families." Each family of fourteen people slept in their own hall, and in the dining room had their own table, and on walks made up their own pairs.

Twice a week we would step beyond our high brick fence. We walked down the small town's streets, by its small brick houses, visited the poor, to present them with clothing we had sewn for them.

We served our monitor duty, and for two weeks I had to clean bedrooms (but not the mattresses). I simply carried clean water up the stairs and dirty water down, and wiped the long washtable where it had been splashed. (I hated that.)

Sometimes we felt like dancing, especially Lucia, who knew how to toss her stem-thin arms high above her arched-back head, her hands like the long transparent lilies that grew in our garden, her legs moving quietly up and down in place. Then, from under her long white shirt, something like the small wings of white turtle-doves would appear and disappear—because we danced at night, on summer nights before the "family" deaconess sisters who slept with us in our bedrooms had arrived.

When the dancing started, they sent for me and for those who were with us.

I remember how often the sight of Lucia, dancing so quietly, so motionlessly, engendered in me an excitement I ill understood. My breathing grew labored, as though all my thoughts, all my delights, my impossible, inconceivable desires had suddenly burst from me at once. Then I leaped from the circle of friends crowded tightly around Lucia and started to dance around her, a sleepwalker, still almost as stone.

I don't know what motions I made, but in them there was evidently something of infectious madness and abandon, that drew with each minute one dancer after another from the crowded circle, throwing them into our whirling, rushing vortex. And since cries and songs were bursting breasts breathless from dancing or contracted in intense observation, and to cry or to sing we knew fatal—so all our cries and all our songs flowed out in the tireless rhythms of muscles contracting, in moans of ecstasy suppressed.

Watchguards were stationed along the whole corridor right to the staircase, and we agreed on certain signs, so that those who danced and those who beheld the dance would be able to get back to their beds in time and dive beneath the blankets. I remember the shuffle of bare feet on the floor then, the fluttering rustle of lightly garbed bodies moving by.

I liked nights after dancing. A kind of calm settled in. Your heart beats and beats like mad, pressed against the pillow, and then grows quiet. Then all my ravenous, vigilant, scrutinizing soul plunges into forgetfulness.

That is rest.

Otherwise there was no rest, either day or night. Because so much was needed, all of it connected and all of it apart. For I did not recover my God, even in school, where sayings from Scripture scolded over every door or were hung or written on the wall: the blessings of the Lord and the Judgment of the Lord, the admonitions of the Lord and His call to us.

I wandered and sought, sought the one I had lost and did not find.

I was silent. And it became terrible—it was so lonely.

I said nothing to Lucia, because I feared that Lucia herself knew. Lucia would die soon. With what unquenched sorrow the lilac rays of her doomed eyes burned. Somehow we all knew she was doomed.

"The doctor has doomed her."

That's how we whispered among her friends, using that word in particular, because it was terrible, mysterious, and beautiful.

I knew that if I told Lucia there was no God she would agree, and there was no way I could bear that. I felt I would lie right down on the floor and scratch at the door with my claws like a dog, start to howl like a dog. That's how terrible it would be.

And I often imagined the terror.

Delicate, dark, pious Gertrude Krone, an orphan educated without tuition by the kind deaconesses, was also my friend. Strictly speaking, she was my only friend, because with Lucia it was something different.

Delicate Gertrude I tormented and loved; with pity she loved me, with adoration. I loved adoration, sought it out. There were no heroics, no audacity too terrible, that I wouldn't have undertaken for the sake of such adoration.

When the whole class looked at the brave girl, taken off to be punished for her heroism, when all faces burned with adoration and worship—the stillness of attainment came upon me, attainment of what was necessary and right.

And of what account was retribution!

In class I tormented Herr Pastor Steffan and Herr Pastor Hattendorf. During class I yelled out, sharp, dry punctuated shouts; it was impossible to catch me:

"Was! Wo! Wie! Wann! Was! Wo! Wie! Wann!"

The offended teacher appealed to the class to hand over the guilty party, but the class kept silent. Once when it happened and the headmistress came in, the terrible, mammoth, righteous-faced Sister Louisa Korten, and accused me—the whole class rose to my defense, first through denial and then with communal tears and sobbing.

On Mondays I snuck the leftover Sunday bread, sprinkled with cinnamon and sugar, out of the storeroom.

If they'd caught me, what infamy!

But loot once in hand—what a radiant triumph! . . . And I set to it with reverence.

The monitor wrote in chalk on the big board the names of those who were naughty before the sister or pastor himself came; I erased the offenders' names and wrote down my own . . .

They ran me out of class.

They assigned me copying exercises.

They didn't take me on walks.

They put me under arrest on the empty third floor.

It was terrible there. And there were spiders.

Strictly speaking, I got to know only three, but if there were three of them, then there were lots, as many as could be. Two of them spun their webs in the window of the empty hall; the third, fastened by a long, quite invisible thread to the ceiling, seemed to be right above my head when I woke the first morning of my first arrest.

I yelled out in a high voice, quite penetrating and distinct, because I was afraid of spiders. Of course, no one came running when I yelled. It wasn't like I was at home; I was on the third floor, under arrest at the deaconesses'.

My cries died out in a long sigh, I grew silent and only then found the strength to turn my head from the pillow and break loose from the spider and the terrible bed.

In the evening before sleep, I dragged the bed out into the middle of the room. During the day I got well acquainted with the two window spiders. They had caught flies in their sticky webs. They ran up to their captives, who sounded an even, thin drone, constant and sickening, and then began busily to circle around them. Each time around, the struggling fly was bound more silently and sturdily, and the droning slowly, evenly disappeared. Soon it was quiet, and the lean, light-footed, lanky creature fastened on without sound or motion.

Then I, too, grew quiet and watched . . .

Once I caught a fly on the window frame and put it in the web myself . . .

They quickly came to the conclusion that I was ruining the dainty Gertrude. The headmistress called me in to see her and forbade me to "go with" her.

That was when our evening meetings began, in a far corner of the corridor, under a black shawl.

That was sweeter still.

At first, Gertrude was timid and refused. She greatly feared her guardians. But still more she feared my adamant eyes. The first nights she came trembling like a dark-eyed young goat, then she came calmly, then she came in love. And we whispered and kissed. We shared with each other the heroics and sorrows of the day. (We were in different classes.) And she often cried and begged me not to love Lucia.

"The doctor said she's doomed. But can't you see, I've got consumption, too? Look how thin and yellow I am."

It made me sorry and envious at the same time. How beautiful to be consumptive! I envied them both, and some malicious feeling provoked strange words.

"Gertrude, you know what? I'll admit to you: I don't love Lucia at all. She's the one who follows me around. I'll show you her note . . . she begs me in it to go with her . . ."

I look for something in my bosom. But, of course, the note's not there, since it doesn't exist.

"Oh I've lost it. What a bother! Gertrude, what am I going to do? It'll be a shame if the 'big girls' find the note. And don't forget that Lucia's a 'big girl,' too. Those idiots will start to hate her for being friends with me."

The comedy succeeds. Through the blissful gleam of dark, devoted eyes, Gertrude is concerned:

"I think maybe you lost it in the garden, when we had gymnastics? Then don't worry, my princess. The gardener sweeps there and no one will find it."

They all thought of me as a princess, a princess in exile, even those to whom I had said that I lived at home in a snow-covered yurt, ate tallow, and rubbed my floor-length hair with warm fat.

"What floor-length hair?"

"They cut it off when they were cleaning me up to send here . . ."

The boredom and listlessness of school began in the morning.

A bell carried down the corridor pierces the brain and frightens the heart.

You're still pulling up the blanket, warm with nighttime's body, over shivering shoulders, you hear your heart jump and you squint sleepy eyes. But from behind the screen comes the perpetually ringing, perpetually waking voice of our family sister, Mathilda.

"Kinder! Kinder! Children, it's already daytime!"

Daytime? It's dark. You poke your nose out—it's cold.

She putters about behind the screen . . . And then there she is, a long-limbed blue figure, with a long face and pale worn-out eyes like a child's, and, on top, the white cap with ruffles, as though she didn't take it off at night.

I jumped out both feet together onto the freezing floor. The monitor lit two wall lamps.

In the middle of the room, almost the whole length of it, stands a washtable. Overnight a thin crust of ice had frozen in the pitchers.

"Wash yourselves well!" commands Sister Mathilda. "Cold water is healthy for the body."

Healthy! What do I care about health? Is Lucia healthy? If only God would grant me to be like her—doomed.

Downstairs the whole school gathers in the dining hall. Lamps under broad iron caps hang over long tables, burning without dispersing the yellowy light in the pale white morning shadows. Rows of coarse white cups with thick rims, chunks of gray bread . . .

Monitors walk about among those seated, pouring thick coffee and boiled milk from tall pitchers.

It's hot! I fall to it greedily. The melancholy is more relentless, the heart more defenseless, from the cold and the shivering. And melancholy keeps growing, still more stubbornly.

I want that which does not exist in this world. In this cold and darkness, in this alien land and loneliness, I want not what is, but what is not.

I gulp the coffee silently, with malice, with hopeless hunger. For the third day now I am carrying a letter from Mama which I've only read half through.

What does Mama write? What can I write her? What matter is it to her, what I don't have?

I have no thoughts, but nor do I have love.

Lucia is over there, far away, at her "family" table. They've also put Gertrude in a different place now . . . away from me . . . so I don't ruin her. Of course, I ruin her. How not, if the Devil is in me.

I would believe in this Devil, I would be ready to believe, if I believed in God . . .

It happened this way, that I found out about him, my very own one. After coffee, we went together in "families" to pray in a special chapel. And during one particular prayer, I had a fit of sneezing; that is, I always knew, really, how to keep from sneezing, it's quite simple: you just hold as much breath in your chest as possible and don't breathe . . . But this time it came out silly and seductive, and for one minute it was clear to me that all the thoughts in all the heads around me had turned from God, and stuck to me.

And I sneezed and sneezed . . .

They let me finish so as not to profane the long prayer with scolding, but when I'd finished and was rushing toward the doors, the loud voice of the majestic headmistress, Sister Louisa Corten, stopped me like a hand on the shoulder:

"Vera, what evil spirit has taken up residence in you?"

Quite beside myself I cried out, with one iniquitous stroke of anger, a distant exile, evil and alone:

"A Russian one."

I was locked up for three days on the third floor. I knit. With the spiders.

They sent a letter home. They brought it to me to write the address.

Of course, that letter didn't get there, since the address turned out not to exist. It came back two months later, but by then the train and the pond had happened, and the rendezvous with Lucia under the shawl.

We came upon the pond on a walk.

Once we set off for the flat fields instead of to the poor. It was a fresh spring day. I walked in a pair with the towheaded, virtuous Agnes Daniels. I despised her and made fun of her with Gertrude; but for the sake of her love and her rapture, I swore her eternal friendship.

The fields were flat and bare, the woods thin, planted in rows, each row like the balding part on Aleksandra Ivanovna's boring head.

We walked down the "part" without joy, without mushrooms, and came out into a new flat field, where yellow mustard bloomed among the winter plantings.

Suddenly the earth ran downward. A small meadow began. They let us go as we liked.

The way the earth tilted downward so suddenly made me greatly excited. I left my friends behind and started running. My heart beat unevenly, my breathing came in fits and starts. I had to do something. I had to. I had to do something.

I ran, coming down hard on one leg along the short, thick grass of the hillside.

Something broke the meadow in two: a straight, even line, with two gleaming strips along it.

And suddenly a shriek, through the whole flat emptiness of the distant, peaceful distance—a wild, long, piercing shriek, flung out in some savage despair. The roaring serpent whirls closer, and I am carried along, already forgetful of myself.

Through the fields, through the fields, through the flat, even fields, through endless woods, along woods that have partings, by tame brick houses with sisters, with sisters, sisters in all of them, endless deaconess sisters; melancholy, peacefulness, stifling kindness—be gone, be gone, take me, oh thundering monster with the smoky tail, along your brilliant path! To the distance, to the distance, to the final, free, uttermost, impossible distance!

I stand by the rail-crossing post. My breast, where my dying heart leaps, bursts out to meet his breast of steel.

Dive beneath the striped beam—and I'm on the rails. There it is, the one that yells so hollow, so wild in my ears, in my soul, into my very breath, so my breath itself might stop! . . .

"Carry me off or kill me . . ."

A whirlwind enclosed me, and the breath of fire and smoke . . .

My hand tore away from the other hand that clasped it. Those doomed eyes looked into mine, and for a moment the violet rays grew dark, while Lucia's face was whiter than the white of her dress. Lips open, speaking, yelling. But could one possibly hear in the howl and rumble of a whirlwind? The fine hair swirls round her head like a gleaming copper cloud.

Then the rumble is farther away, the whirlwind quieter. The howl breaks suddenly into sobbing, and I hear it in snatches:

"Already last time I wanted to. But when I saw you . . . I guessed, when you were running, that you would want to, too . . ."

Suddenly, with horror, I understood what it was we had longed for just now . . . We—she and I. And that the train had rushed past, that it had rushed on, and that we stood alone now in the field, the two of us, both doomed. And the rails gleam into the distance . . . Then I opened my mouth and absurdly, not like at home, began to howl.

Shaking all over, her face unfamiliar, convulsed with malice, Lucia hit me in the chest. And ran back to her friends.

I walked farther in silence, very quiet, avoiding Lucia and Gertrude and Agnes.

But when we had come to the pond (yes, that faint, languid meadow sloped down to a pond) and I saw how the silken ripples spread out brilliantly along the flat surface of emerald gray water, rocking quietly, rustling, whispering on the stones of the wet meadow shore—I could no longer stop.

I walked. And walked. Walked that way until the calm, decisive water rose and embraced me to the waist, until I first heard the long scream and cries on the shore . . .

How hard it was to drag wet skirts on your body! And my shoes squished.

Lucia didn't approach me. Lucia despised me. Gertrude came up to me and asked timidly:

"Why did you run into the pond?"

"It's not a pond."

"Then what is it?"

"It's the sea."

And a minute later, once I'd overcome all my heavy, fluid sadness, I almost yelled:

"It's the sea! The sea!"

Did Lucia despise me?

But that night Lucia said to me:

"Why do you go with little Gertrude? She's stupid."

I answered, without knowing why:

"Just because . . . to annoy you."

Lucia got angry.

"You're forgetting who I am! I could have lots of friends more interesting than you."

"Sure, but you don't love the 'older girls,' you love me."

I said it insolently, and it seemed to me now that everything was lost, and that it was even better that way, completely . . . so be it . . .

Lucia grew quiet . . . suddenly sorrowful, tender, and frightened, she threw both thin, slight, dryly burning arms round my neck, then drew back and looked into my eyes, rays of lilac burning in her tear-filled eyes.

That evening, Lucia agreed to come to our corner (mine and Gertrude's), where the corridor was dark beside the night window.

And I invited Gertrude, too, whispering quickly after our long morning prayer together, in a crowd by the door . . . But to her I said:

"Look, don't wait in the old corner, but in the one across, by the hall stand."

She waited, her narrow body too tall for her twelve years, so warm and supple always beneath the shawl, squeezed tight in the opposite corner . . . Today Gertrude will see how Lucia loves me . . . She'll stand alone in the empty corner and watch.

I had the black shawl. And I walked along holding Lucia's hand.

That evening, under the shawl, I told Lucia everything. It happened because we remembered the train and the pond, and because Lucia herself seemed mad, so that as she walked up she didn't even notice Gertrude, and because we kissed beneath the shawl with some kind of mortal, painful languor, as though we were . . . doomed.

Of course we were doomed. She to death and I to destruction . . . So that's why I told her everything about God—how there is no God, how nothing exists, that it's impossible.

Lucia wasn't surprised. Of course it all worked out the way I knew it would. The ultimate horror. Doomed to impending death, Lucia already knew there was no God. And we pressed against each other in a kind of embrace, exhausting and intense, as though somehow, somehow that might bring forgetfulness.

We didn't give a thought to Gertrude and to where she'd gone.

It was only at morning coffee that we learned now Gertrude had been horribly punished. During the night they looked for her in her hall and found her in the garden, gone quite wild. For two weeks we didn't see her. She was under arrest.

The headmistress called me from evening class, the day after the pond and the meeting, and explained, severely, that I was ruining Gertrude. The spirit of eternal rebellion lives in me, it looks out of my eyes, my movements, it cries out in my every word, it's the spirit of the Devil, no matter who I approach, they sense it. It's the weak who let him in. That's how it is with Gertrude. If they ever find us together, if they discover we're writing letters, even exchanging glances—Gertrude will be immediately expelled and sent to her guardians.

Expel Gertrude! Not me but her! Now that astonished me. And I looked at the adamant eyes of the splendid, righteous-faced Sister Louisa Corten with powerful disdain.

In class, after walk time, we spent the three hours till supper doing lessons. From the headmistress I went back there to my friends, who had been frightened for me; I sat in my seat and started to cry.

What else was I to do? Every other action of mine would reflect not on me but on Gertrude. From now on, no matter what I did in defense of her and our friendship, it would reflect not on me but on her.

And I cried, crushed for the first time by the dispassionate falsehood of life.

The weight of constraint lay on my back, pressed my head down to the desk. Head buried in my handkerchief, I cried and couldn't stop.

Three hours later the bell for evening tea sounded in the corridor, and my friends took me by the arm to our hall, to bed; I was completely crushed, my face swollen and my legs weak . . .

Because I loved my delicate Gertrude, pitifully, indelibly . . .

And when she came back down to us from the spiders' floor, I wrote her my first note in blood.

From that time on, we wrote letters in blood and found message carriers to serve us, given the mortal danger.

I fell in love with Sister Louisa Rino. She had incredibly big, gray-blue eyes, round and intense, and a full childish mouth, just like a cherubim's.

And since the secret I had shared no longer bound my tongue, but still burned my heart as before, I told her what I knew about God. Now it was even more probable—that He did not exist.

This infatuation passed quickly, because I didn't like being betrayed: she betrayed me to Sister Louisa Corten herself.

Once more, the tall headmistress called me in, but she spoke in a tender and inviting voice, and sat me down in a chair beside her in her severe study.

"Your thoughts have entered the minds of many, even the great," she concluded her speech, "they doubted God's existence, but His greatness was always revealed to them and mercy called them."

And she handed me a book. And let me miss classes for two days. She enjoined me to read and to give myself over to reflection.

In the empty garden along the far brick fence, while my friends were studying with the Herr Pastors, I wandered back and forth, and read how Voltaire, when he saw the marvelous sunrise, fell to his knees and blessed the Creator.

I did not bless Him.

I started surreptitiously spilling the washpail on the stair, and then, at the usual cleaning time, I'd pour clean water into it and take it down as usual. That was a cover. So no one would catch me. But even without catching me at it they knew, and I knew they knew, and I started to do everything backward, the way I shouldn't.

And then, on one of those nights, the Devil appeared to me.

I wanted to save myself and couldn't. My soul was empty and aching. Before I had known only my own unjust desires; now I felt the whole of life was unjust, that there was no justice.

I was afraid. And then the Devil appeared to me.

In the night a killing melancholy came over me. I was alone. They had taken Lucia to the hospital. She had had an attack of choking, and blood poured out of her throat. I didn't dare walk with Gertrude. Agnes Daniels had somehow learned of my betrayal and had indignantly rejected me. I hated Sister Louisa Rino and tormented her with my insolence.

I didn't want a new love. To love means to betray. Can a heart that has learned to betray break out of its solitude? I felt repulsive and hopeless.

And through all the dreary, mortal melancholy that enveloped my heart, I had a feeling of joy.

I jumped on the bed and looked into the shining darkness beyond the window.

You couldn't see the moon, but the air itself seemed saturated with its rays and trembled slowly like liquid.

My joy increased. My wild joy increased, and inside me it trembled, liquid, swelling. Sharp, malicious, alluring.

Alone? Thank God! Malicious? Thank God again! A traitor? Thank God again!

Everything that is clenched tight, completely contemptuous, deft, and courageous, strong against pain and pity and shame—that is me! That is me!

And thank God.

Somewhere beyond the window shone the moon, and I felt ill at ease because I couldn't see where it was, I saw only the light, which trembled slowly, like liquid. And it seemed to go rolling over me, rolling on and bearing me with it toward the window, through the window, into some wholly empty, terrible space, quite new . . .

The light became frightening to me. I no longer knew whether I was dreaming or awake. I knew only one thing, that I must hold tight, tight, squeezing with all my muscles onto the bed, so as not to float off, not to float off on those waves, those awful, even waves of incoherent green light, quicksilver waves that led toward the window, through the window, into the new, the too large, the too empty, where I would suffocate, where I would suffocate, where right now, this very minute, I would suffocate.

I look through the window and my heart draws back. The Devil is there. He is scratching the glass with iron nails. I start laughing: I'm not afraid of anything.

Then what did I take fright at?

And I jumped from the bed and ran toward that shadow, the one bent beyond the window; it was cold—bare feet on the floor—and joyful—with a resolute spirit.

I pushed at the window frame. You can't shake him off! He's tenacious. He's very tenacious, sticky. He sticks to things.

I sit close to him on the windowsill. But he's already down below. There, by the pine tree, beneath the window, his shadow is there in the shadow of the pine.

Or did I dream it? Was it all a dream? But then where did the dream come from? Did it start when God didn't exist? Or when the Devil started scratching? Or had it started when I was still good? Then everything was a dream, the whole thing was only a dream? Then it didn't matter if you were happy or sad, if there was good or evil, or even if there was God or the Devil?

What if you jumped . . .

There, below. You wouldn't kill yourself. It's only two stories.

Then why had I been afraid of the train?

"Vera! Vera!"

The perpetually ringing, perpetually vigilant voice called me from behind the screen.

The fresh night breeze had no doubt drifted in beyond the screen there from the window, because the window was open, and I was sitting huddled on the windowsill; now it was certain I was awake and not dreaming.

I think it was the next day that the letter was returned, the one the headmistress had written Mama, that hadn't been delivered, since the address wasn't right.

And that morning, even before the fateful mail came, I met Gertrude on the stairway and suddenly yelled out at her in a wild frenzy:

"Today I'll drive them all mad, the swine!"

She was under the stairway—Rino.

They took me up to the third floor and sent home a telegram that I'd been expelled.

My older brother came for me and took me to Italy, to the sea, where he planned to spend the autumn with his family. I was to live there for several weeks until they'd found me a new school in Germany.

They drove me off at dawn, half an hour before the morning bell. No one knew, not Gertrude, not Lucia in her infirmary, that we drove by in the blind whiteness of morning.

I didn't cry. I was like a tightly corked bottle. It's so stupid: it's full to the top, it doesn't even shake, but you can't figure out what's in the bottle. I didn't even know myself: malice? repentance? fear? joy? despair? Or was it simply death, that final death I was fated to, to which of course Lucia was also fated, because she "knew"?

On the road, all the way to Italy, my brother didn't talk to me, just as he hadn't when we met, when he didn't kiss me, just extended his hand. Actually, he asked one question: was it true that I'd poured dirty water in the corridor, and when he found out I had he turned from me with sorrow and shame; another time, as we sat at a table d'hôte, he suggested I should use clean handkerchiefs.

That was all.

At the sea, in Italy, I lived in silence with his silent, industrious, beautiful wife, with her young sons. Sometimes I looked into her eyes and averted my gaze in fear. I had been in love with her before, when I was still quite young, when she was engaged to my brother. I hadn't dared kiss her nimble white hands. Once I stole a slipper of garnet velvet that she wore in the morning, and at night beneath the pillow I kissed it, warm and smelling of rubber.

Then she was swift as the wind in our town apartment, a teaser, cheerful, quick-tempered; her long hair twined above a calm, clear forehead.

Now in her large, bright eyes, beneath their sternly arched russet brows, I saw but one order, one request, as her faint lashes shuddered suddenly: "keep quiet."

And her white hands had grown strong and slow, powerful and exacting:

"Work; work," their stern features said to me.

"And do not ask! Do not ask! And have patience, have patience!" said the delicate wrinkles on the young, stern brow.

"You know your duty. Keep quiet. Keep quiet."

Brother's family was happy and friendly. Silently friendly. Benevolently strict . . . industrious.

I didn't like to play with my nephews. I didn't like to play with "little kids." If you play horses you can't beat them.

So I went alone to the sea.

It was deep blue, the high rocks almost black, and the black, scattered shingle was moistened by waves, sprinkled with foamy white.

I sat down on the shore, where the sun beat down, right by the water. I sat.

I didn't think. What was there to think about? If you start thinking, everything is nasty.

Of course, everyone was right and I wasn't. The saintly deaconettes, or rather the deaconesses, had expelled me for theft, lying, deceit, for a devilish spirit. Of course, they were saintly.

Well, what did it matter. Let them.

Could there be saints, if there was no God?

That was funny. Then anyone can become a saint. Anyone who wants to. It's rubbish, about the deaconesses being saints, they're not real ones.

But you can also become a real one. Whoever wants to can make themselves into a saint. I know that. It's as simple as the fact that now I'm damned.

And anyone can be damned, if only they want to be—that's true and as simple and clear as becoming a saint. The joy is just the same.

At any rate, I can, because I always go to the limit, I'll twist myself there, I'll turn myself there, I'll dance till I'm there.

There's just one thing: if it's so certain that you can be a saint or be damned (and then, too, it's probable, since there *were* saints and damned: everyone studies that and knows it), then how can there be no God?

If it's hot—then there's fire. If there's ice—then there's frost. If there's a saint—then there's God. If you're damned—then there's a Devil.

Enough. I didn't want to think. There are no saints and no damned. There are simply stupid minutes. Just like that, one after another, each separate. If there were saints, even just one, any old one, just one, only a real one, only the most real kind—then everyone would be with him now, everyone would be with him this very minute and for all minutes, and all the minutes would be one.

That means there wasn't even one. Not any real one.

So I was alone, and the minute was alone.

There is the slap, slap of wave upon wave, and each crest burbles: "I am alone. I am alone. I am alone."

"One—a minute, two—a minute, three—a minute . . ."

The hour-wavelets will tick away until it's time for me to run home. But still it's better to sit here, like this, alone.

I had shamed the whole family.

My mama's over there.

And where is Aleksandra Ivanovna?

Volodya had written yesterday. But I hadn't read it. He no doubt was playing by himself.

Ruslan . . . What stupidity. It's not worth it now.

The sun is too hot. I clamber into the shadow of the rocks. Something makes a thin, ringing noise, sickening, without interruption.

Could there be spiders even here?

The ringing itches at my heart. If only it would tire! If only it would beat its little wings more gently.

Oh, it's not a spider but a bit of water. There's a narrow stream somewhere in the rocks. Now I understand. Suddenly I feel easier, as though a weight's been lifted from a smothered heart, and I can't say why but suddenly I have faith, the faintest bit of faith that it's all a dream, all a dream, and I'll wake up at home.

Home . . .

Home, with God there and everyone together.

It grew dull in the shadow behind the rock face. The rock face is completely in the water there, and it's cool from the water, of course.

From a new rock I see how the sun plays like golden mesh on the water, so intensely blue. The rocks on the bottom have come to life—the backs of large turtles are gilded, schools of fish are living silver streams.

Quite close—because the water off these rocks was now deep—a joyous dolphin jumped, its round face like a child's. It has a kind, round face.

I lean closer to the water.

Under the water, my rock is covered over with moss. No, it's not moss, it's alive, too—mushrooms with living fringes, bright blue and scarlet, they close and open to meet the oncoming waves, and in the malachite moss there are snail shells exposed . . . trustingly, to the rising tide.

Something moved black beneath the water, along the flat rock woven in sunny, golden mesh. A crab! How funny! He moves sideways, all feet and claws, but knows where he's going. There's a long, narrow crevice. The crab has dived into it . . . That means the crevice isn't empty. A gleaming black round crab, a round one with claws, lives in it.

And the mesh quivers, lapping its golden threads. I hear a rustling of threads. The splash of gentle surf on pebbles, the rustle of a gritty wave as it recedes.

I've been sitting for some time now, watching the living sea. The thickening blue of the water is covered now with a new bluish-gray, a bluish-gray film of silver along the golden mesh.

It's noon.

Hot. It's empty on the shore.

I go for a swim.

It's not worth running home for a swimsuit. The boys will insist on coming with me. My brother's wife will warn me not to be late for dinner. I'll go this way. Too bad that it's scary to take off your shirt.

Or can you? I'll swim out deeper.

I swim there with the small fish, with the living mushrooms, with the snails, with the dolphin, with the crab . . . There on the bottom there are sea urchins, black with sharp lime stubble.

I see them through the silver-blue glassy depth. They, too, seem dark purple, like the terrible dark blotches that are groves of underwater grass. It's good that I'm swimming. If you needed to step on the shingle, then you might get a splinter in your foot from the rocky stubble of urchins on the bottom, you might get tangled in the purple-brown, palm-shaped stalks, all bubbled . . .

I swim far out. Farther than where I saw the dolphin with the childlike face. Here, when you look into the glimmering depth, the water is already green, the sun in it thick yellow, like amber. The shadows of submarine cliffs fan out, immense, incomprehensible.

There aren't any sharks in the rocks, are there? Or large, big-bellied cuttlefish? They could suck me into their stomachs with soft tentacles, you can't pull them off . . .

And if for a moment you dip your head under the water and close your eyes—sound is muffled, muffled, the heavy streaked light is obscured, then it's not frightening anymore . . . it's not frightening to die . . .

The salt water supports you effortlessly. You can turn on your back, squint your eyes from the enormous light.

Purple twilight, and the silence is all purple.

I lie without moving.

Where is the invisible current carrying me?

Do I really need to know where?

But thoughts of sharks stir stupid fears.

I'm already on shore, on the even, scattered shingle . . . I want to pull the shirt over my wet body. But I wait a bit, lazing and languid. I'm not afraid. Who will come along the empty beach at the dead of noon?

Hot. By now it's very hot. And there's no protection for my head. In the morning I'd run away from the "horses" and forgotten my hat. It felt jumbled in my head. It's probably the sun beating mercilessly on my skull.

I jump up. I run to the high black rocks. I'm looking for shade. By now there's none. The sun races after me and turns my head, light-headed fear starts a pounding in my rushing heart.

There's a slit between rocks. I crawl in without thinking, scraping my shoulder as I squeeze in, because my head is spinning and my breathing is fitful.

There's a small cave in the depth of the crevice. It's damp, quiet, dark. My head and shoulders are already in. Then all of me.

I lie silent. I'm happy.

Maybe the crab has a cave in his crevice, too?

I lie, squinting my eyes. I must be smiling. It's fine in the cool, damp quiet.

My eyes have opened. The flat black rock is near my eyes. That's the wall of my cave. I like to look at things that way, very close up.

Suddenly I notice something moving. It's because my eyes are so close to the flat wall that I can see such small movement. A small red spider is crawling from down below, from the pebbles up the wall. All of him is no bigger than a tiny scarlet bead. But I see him clearly. I see his four small eyes on the small head. Four gleaming points that stick out.

Of course that's his eyes.

Suddenly the little spider stops abruptly, right at the level of my eyes. It's not moving. I look into his four small eyes, the four eyes on the small scarlet bead. And suddenly I sense it: those four small red spider's eyes are seeing my eyes, immeasurable as the sea, like two seas without shores . . . and those four immeasurably tiny eyes are looking into my two limitless eyes, looking and measuring, fearing and pondering.

A moment, two, three . . .

I hold my breath and wait for his decision. And abruptly, the small red spider turned the little bead downward, slipped along the wet wall into his pebbly shingle, from where he'd come.

Quietly, quietly, carefully I move my stiff body out from the chilly cave.

The red spider lives there, in the little cave. He fears me.

Why frighten him? Why peer uninvited at his life, his decisions?

I sat quietly. Quietly I drew on my underwear and dress.

I went to the water to dampen my scarf, to cover my head with the damp scarf.

I didn't put my shoes on. My steps are firm; I touch the wet stones with caressing feet, stones that have been smoothed by caressing waves, stones that are wet and warm beneath the burning heat of the sun.

I picked one up, a striped one, smelled it and licked it: salty, warm, wet.

I remember that I started to cry—why, I didn't know. I hadn't cried that way for a long time . . .

And suddenly everything grew baffling . . . I lay down on the shingle. I dug into it with bare feet, clung to it with my face. Warm, wet . . . The blood pounding dully in my ears, dark and muffled, warm and wet, resonant, then silence.

Oh God—I am a little stone!

I am myself a wet, warmed stone, quiet beneath the resonating wave. And the purple darkness is within me as well . . . And I am the small red spider—the crimson beadlet with four pointlet-eyes. It is damp and cool in my cave. And I am the black crab, sideways, speeding sideways . . . And the mushrooms with the fringe . . . the submarine water is flowing, I sense it, I know it, I open the fringe to it—I catch distant currents. I hear; I hear the great depth, the distant, muffled depth, very quiet and thick.

I kiss the stones and lick them with my tongue again: they're salty. Is it my tears? Or the sea water? It's salty, too.

Is the sea crying, too?

Or is the sea all tears, the tears of rocks and spiders, and of crabs, and mine, the tears of the earth?

I feel good, of course, and something has yielded, something that had become unbearable.

For a long time I hadn't cried. For too long . . . that way, for joy.

Will

Dedicated to Sergei Gorodetsky *

About that time Alena Simkina was supposed to give birth.

In childhood, she and I had carted potatoes on her mother's wagon from the dirty autumn fields; I would run off without my governess knowing. Now we were both eighteen. Last spring she had married Simkin from Shirokovo, who was just her age and had lost both parents.

As older girls we hadn't seen each other, but had heard about her marriage and the impending birth from Maria Frantsevna, the country medic, whom I loved, with flutterings of poetry and devotion—she was indefatigable and strapping, with a bright womanly smile on her manly face.

That morning something sent me off to see Alena. I gathered a bundle of old linen for baby clothes and bedding for the baby she was expecting and hauled it to the stables myself, to hurry Fedor along with the harnessing.

But it turned out Fedor wasn't home: he and the groom were exercising a new team of four. I had to lead my Cossack from the paddock myself and harness him to the charabanc.

---

* Sergei Gorodetsky (1884–1967) was a poet and cofounder of the Acmeist movement in Russian poetry; his first volume of verse appeared in 1907, the year *The Tragic Menagerie* was published.

I jumped into the carriage flushed and resolute, tossed in my bundle, and led Cossack out of the barn. The horseshoes clattered, and the wheels went rumbling down the planks toward the gravel-surfaced road.

The spring grove let through light like pale yellow lace. The swollen, rich earth thrust up the first tiny rays of green grass. Space stretched open. It smelled of roots, of the steamy rot of leaves, of resinous splashing buds, and once of fantastic, unusually early sweet buttercup.

The grove ended. The gray countryside began, flooded with shining silver puddles. Then a single-track village road cut a narrow straight line across black fields, brown fallow land, and bright green strips of low winter crops.

It was empty and space stretched open; the fragrant wind carried far, and beyond the nakedness of black breathing earth the sharply burning sun glinted in distant, empty sky. I longed for heroic deeds, and for love. I dropped the reins and stopped guiding Cossack, and my charabanc rocked back and forth, diving from one pothole to another on the shaky track. It threw me bodily from one side to the other, and it was good.

I longed for heroic deeds, and for love. The heroism of sacrificing one's life; love that was passion. And I wanted them together, and together, right now.

I pressed the lids of my eyes. My lashes met, trembling. Then the whole expanse of springtime started to sparkle, and the whole of my will sped on sparkling paths toward the horizon bow, where dark blue forest met the empty, pale blue of sky in the distant distance. And everything became possible, became my own. And it is this that I have never forgotten, how my heart grew ruthless and my will grew unyielding, as a bowstring strung tight.

A jolt . . . As though I'd been hit in the back, and I struck my chest on the front of the charabanc. My horse thrashed up to his chest in viscous mud, and the springtime swill poured around my legs above the sunken wheels.

The streams.

Of course: every spring there are these streams just before Shirokovo. Last spring, Semyon drowned here. In springtime it floods. You can't hold back the earth in spring, it's like a quagmire with no bottom. The earth opens.

Cossack struggles. I stand in the charabanc up to my ankles in mud, holding the reins high, whooping loudly, joyfully, wildly. And one thought alone keeps running through my quite calm head: will he pull it out, or won't he? Will he pull it out, or won't he?

The wheels moved. You can't see them. Are they floating? Or on the bottom? And Cossack, with his ears pressed flat, black now instead of bay, alternately ducking his back and thrusting his crupper up—is he swimming? Or on the bottom? . . . with a choking whoop, I greet the evil spring, while sharp burning rays glint blindingly on the viscous, bottomless mud.

A knock. It's the wheel hitting something hard. The small charabanc pitched to the other side. Will it topple over? But it doesn't. We made it out.

In Shirokovo the small black huts are drowning in spring muck. Four, five, six . . . There's Alena's hut. Cossack carefully heaves the charabanc onto the brown hill, slippery with grass.

I toss the reins over the fence post and already I'm in the entranceway. The muddy bundle, all wet through, stayed in the charabanc.

After the blinding openness, I grope with difficulty in the half-light for the door handle.

I grasped it, pushed.

Lots of women in the hut. They step back.

On the floor, on the hay—a body. The legs are bent sharply up at naked knees. The head is thrust back. The face is gray as earth. The mouth gapes horribly. Yawning wide.

"We don't know, has she died?"

Something in the corner bleated pitifully.

"Did she have the child?"

"She was born three days ago. After that she was burning up. She kept yelling, 'Save me.' We didn't know what was wrong . . . The womenfolk fussed over her, but it was no good."

"Where's the doctor?"

"He's off somewhere in the county."

"And Maria Frantsevna?"

"She took Andriusha Kozel to the clinic in town; they're going to cut him open . . ."

There were more strange words, but it's hard to understand how your friend has died at eighteen, how she's turned to earth . . .

It's not light in the hut, and it's stuffy. There are women by the small low window. There are women by the oven, so huge it takes up half the room. They're crowded by the door.

Above the bench by the window hangs Alena's small mirror in a tin frame. She was so thin, so pale when we hauled potatoes together, on her mother Maria's wagon . . .

I brought the small mirror to her black mouth. No vapor on the rippled glass: she's not breathing. The face is like earth, ageless; the mouth is black as the muck and mud.

Something bleated pitifully in the corner.

"She's gone."

The womenfolk turned to the icons, lifting submissive eyes, dropping low submissive heads, tracing broad, submissive crosses on chests and over shoulders.

My eyes watched unsubmissively, my unyielding will stretched within me like a bowstring. For myself I awaited heroic deeds and sacrifice.

But *she* was dead!

And bending low to the straw, I closed the lids on the secret in her immensely startled eyes . . .

"Where is Simkin?"

"He hasn't come back yet from carting . . ."

"Take the fallows around the streams."

Yes, of course; I forgot about it just now. So I skirt the hut and then ride through the old fields, their ground more solid, where the hooves make a disgusting squishing noise as they tread the brown earth. The reins in my hand, I clutch a small bundle with the tightly swaddled child close to my breast. No one there could keep it themselves. The spring rush is beginning.

Once again it is empty and open. The fragrant wind rushes on. And above the nakedness of black, breathing earth the sharply burning sun is gleaming in empty, distant sky. I long for heroic deeds . . . and for victory.

They await me, the challenge and the victory. I will leave this life of contentment and good behavior. I will leave those near and dear. Even Cossack I will leave . . . forever without my horse, with only my will. From town Maria Frantseva will bring a letter from her comrade. He has everything ready. His brother has already resolved on suicide. In the next few days he will shoot himself, but before that he will marry me, to set me free from the ones here.*

* The scenario Vera imagines was the stuff of both fact and fiction in late-nineteenth-century Russia. "Fictitious marriage" helped liberate noble girls from conventional lives, with the aid of idealistic young men, willing to be "bridegrooms" for a day.—TRANS.

And then I will join my dear friend, and we will go off together in search of heroic deeds! His brother is, in any case, not long for this world; he has no will. The bow of his life is not drawn by will. We will draw it for him, for three, for everyone we'll draw it, for the whole world we'll draw it ! Like that arching distance . . .

His wife! . . . that is, my friend's wife?

She . . . No, she is not one of us. She is not with us. In the rear of life . . . She is like Alena, like the suicide brother, like a victim without heroic purpose . . .

Oh, inexhaustible will, draw taut! You who are dead, are dead; I live.

If I must die—I will die for you, for him, for the world.

Let death come! Life and death are of equal worth to me. Life and death are equal in their ecstasy.

I live for you. I die for you.

My sister . . . I am myself . . . my world.

The wife of our estate manager cannot give birth. Three times they've pounded an infant's head, four days of torment. Three days ago it happened again.

I was taking the child to her, to her full, unneeded breast.

"Verochka, love, Verochka, my breast is useless!"

She had said it to me yesterday in such a weak whisper, and had wept so touchingly. She will kiss my hands for the gift, and the wrinkled face of the suckling child.

It bleated pitifully in my bundle.

Something touched my forehead gently, tickled my cheek warmly and fluttered down. A feather! . . . Two bits of fluff. The wind caught them up and carried them somewhere, off into empty space.

Where were they from?

I threw back my head.

High in the empty shimmering gleams a falcon, its wings unmoving.

The two bits of fluff can't be his, of course . . .

He burns like a spark in the blue . . .

Heart, grow hot to meet the rays of sun!

Heart, you are stronger than sun, triumphant will: heart of mine, heart of the world, heart let fall to earth by God!

From the knoll we descended to the road, on the other side now of the streams. I stand in the charabanc, my left forearm gently and firmly holding the bundled child to my breast.

I lifted the reins high, and let out a whoop.

Cossack stretched out like an arrow. Cossack forgot the trot. Cossack is a cossack and gallops like an arrow. The charabanc pounds along the ruts of uneven track.

The nursling child is quiet. The hungry nursling has rocked to sleep on my pitching, rolling breast.

Drunken will of an evil spring, I have not forgotten you!

European Classics

M. Ageyev
Novel with Cocaine

Jerzy Andrzejewski
Ashes and Diamonds

Honoré de Balzac
The Bureaucrats

Andrei Bely
Kotik Letaev

Heinrich Böll
Absent without Leave
And Never Said a Word
And Where Were You, Adam?
The Bread of Those Early Years
End of a Mission
Irish Journal
Missing Persons and Other Essays
The Safety Net
A Soldier's Legacy
The Stories of Heinrich Böll
Tomorrow and Yesterday
The Train Was on Time
What's to Become of the Boy?
Women in a River Landscape

Madeleine Bourdouxhe
La Femme de Gilles

Karel Čapek
Nine Fairy Tales
War with the Newts

Lydia Chukovskaya
Sofia Petrovna

Grazia Deledda
After the Divorce
Elias Portolu

Leonid Dobychin
The Town of N

Yury Dombrovsky
The Keeper of Antiquities

Aleksandr Druzhinin
Polinka Saks • The Story of Aleksei Dmitrich

Venedikt Erofeev
Moscow to the End of the Line

Konstantin Fedin
Cities and Years

Arne Garborg
Weary Men

Fyodor Vasilievich Gladkov
Cement

I. Grekova
The Ship of Widows

Vasily Grossman
Forever Flowing

Stefan Heym
The King David Report

Marek Hlasko
The Eighth Day of the Week

Bohumil Hrabal
Closely Watched Trains

Ilf and Petrov
The Twelve Chairs

Vsevolod Ivanov
Fertility and Other Stories

Erich Kästner
Fabian: The Story of a Moralist

Valentine Kataev
Time, Forward!

Kharms and Vvedensky
*The Man with the Black Coat: Russia's
Literature of the Absurd*

Danilo Kiš
*The Encyclopedia of the Dead
Hourglass*

Ignacy Krasicki
The Adventures of Mr. Nicholas Wisdom

Miroslav Krleza
The Return of Philip Latinowicz

Curzio Malaparte
*Kaputt
The Skin*

Karin Michaëlis
The Dangerous Age

Neera
Teresa

V. F. Odoevsky
Russian Nights

Andrey Platonov
The Foundation Pit

Bolesław Prus
*The Sins of Childhood and
Other Stories*

Valentin Rasputin
Farewell to Matyora

Alain Robbe-Grillet
Snapshots

Arthur Schnitzler
The Road to the Open

Yury Trifonov
Disappearance

Evgeniya Tur
Antonina

Ludvík Vaculík
The Axe

Vladimir Voinovich
*The Life and Extraordinary Adventures
of Private Ivan Chonkin
Pretender to the Throne*

Lydia Zinovieva-Annibal
The Tragic Menagerie

Stefan Zweig
Beware of Pity